I0666343

Love, Torture, and Redemption

First Edition

Christopher Trevor

Love, Torture, and Redemption

First Edition

Published by The Nazca Plains Corporation
Las Vegas, Nevada
2007

ISBN: 978-1-887895-32-3

Published by

The Nazca Plains Corporation ®
4640 Paradise Rd, Suite 141
Las Vegas NV 89109-8000

© 2007 by The Nazca Plains Corporation. All rights reserved.
No part of this work may be reproduced or utilized in any form
or by any means, electronic or mechanical, including photocopy-
ing, microfilm, and recording, or by any information storage and
retrieval system, without permission in writing from the publisher.
Printed in the United States of America.

PUBLISHER'S NOTE
Love, Torture, and Redemption is a work of fiction created wholly
by *Christopher Trevor's* imagination. All characters are fictional
and any resemblance to any persons living or deceased is purely
by accident. No portion of this book reflects any real person or
events.

Cover, Greasetank
Art Director, Blake Stephens

Dedication

Charlie: thanks for helping me to find an ending to this saga…
(Jump for My Love!!!)

Acknowledgments

To: First and foremost Joe T: a unique artist: for early votes of confidence back in the gay 90s.

To: Etienne: another unique artist, but gone too soon. Your erotic drawings are a true inspiration to what I write about.

To: Ron: the boss man, for honesty and for fueling my erotic imagination. Thanks for adding fuel to the fire boss man.

To: Neil: thanks for being my feet mentor and now my writing critic.

To: The two construction workers on the early morning train whose names I never knew, but you guys became Master Kent and Bobby in my outlandish imagination...

To: John Embry and the staff from the long ago magazines, "Drummer" and "Manifest Reader", for positioning me on this perilous journey and helping me to see it through...

To: Tim Brough: for artistic and fiendish inspiration. Thanks for being there at my first book signing table and for teaching me the ropes...so to speak...

To: The "TRUE" Leather men that I have had the honor and privilege of meeting: thank you for support and for teaching me about your magnificent and riveting way of life.

To: Alan, my partner, for patience and for putting up with the 2:00 AM writings.

Love, Torture, and Redemption

First Edition

Christopher Trevor

Contents

A Boner Book

Author's Notes
about his most famous story:

"The Taking of Master's Boy", which has now become "Love, Torture, Redemption."

Before my first two books were officially published, they being "The Executive Guide to Foot Fetishism and Office Discipline" and "Executive Ties That Bind" my publisher asked me which of my short stories my favorite was. In other words, which story did I think I would be remembered for the most? I instantly replied by saying, "The Taking of Master's Boy." The story was first published by "Manifest Reader" magazine back in the 1990's and I would have to say that it truly is one of my most riveting stories. When it first appeared in "Manifest Reader" a notion got about by some people that I had been done away with, in other words, that I had lost my mind. Some people who read it before it saw the light of day maintained that it was overly graphically violent and that the work that had started as a short story had gone beyond the writer's control. I do admit that the characters of Robert (Bobby) and Master Kent were based on real people (although I do not know them formally) and the story basically wrote itself, especially toward the end of part four. One or two people who read the story could not believe that it was I who had written it. I am essentially a very conservative, laid back and quiet person. To quote my best friend Jeff, he said, "Christopher, if I did not know that you were the author of this story I would never think that you had written it." I see those words as a definite compliment to what I do and what I create as a writer.

Another friend, Eric, pointed out the limitations of the human body and just how much Bobby would have been able to realistically endure. Other friends argued that no man could endure such horrific violence and come away not needing to go to a hospital. It was not, as some people said, very credible. I on the other hand always thought it was. After thinking over all the things that have been said about this particular story, both good, bad, in between and otherwise I am indebted to everyone for all the feedback they offered me and that I ever got because of it. It seems that the leather guys loved it most of all. My artist buddy, Joe T. said, "Very, very good story Christopher," when he read the finished product. It is but one story that I wrote out of many others. Because it truly touches on more than one nerve I would think is the reason that it garnered so much attention when it was published. In regards to reader's endurance, the postulate must be accepted that the story *was and always will be* interesting somehow. It is the necessary preliminary assumption.

If I had not believed in it, if I had not believed that it was a raw and interesting fantasy story to tell I could never have begun to write it in the first place. As to all the questions of the physical endurances that Bobby suffers in the story I again say, it's a fantasy. We all know that in real life Bobby would have either passed out or needed to be rushed to an emergency room, or, more sadly he might have even died from the constant psychological terror that was being heaped on him alongside the physical humiliating abuse he was suffering. I, as the author admit that this is one of the most graphic "Cleeve and Otis" stories that I ever wrote. Besides all this I have kept in mind all the responses this story received. I did a book signing recently at a GMSMA event and some of the leathermen there knew of my story, "The Taking of Master's Boy." We, as the masses, have to presume that there must have been something in this particular story that forced most people, whether they hated it or not to read it all the way through to the not so happy ending for Police Officer John McLaughlin. I am known for my not so happy and twisted yet comical endings. But in all seriousness, the truth of the matter is, that my first thought was of a short story, concerned only with Bobby's capture and eventual return to Master Kent by Cleeve and Otis. And I have to say that in my mind that was a legitimate conception. But the way I decided to end it opened up the doors for a sequel or two or three. Everyone wanted to know what happened to the poor cop. Then the other obvious question; how did Master Kent and Bobby meet? Hence, the third installment of this story where that is detailed by Master Kent himself. After writing the first installment I realized that I had the makings of a novel here. A very good and old friend of mine, Charlie, who read it recently for the first time came up with the brilliant idea for the fourth installment which takes place twenty years later. That end of the story was finally written when the request for the novel was made. All the reactions, all the questions, all the heart poundings this story caused for people are all compliments to the achievement that I think I made in allowing my inner self and my deepest imagination to run wild. The first few pages I laid aside were not without their weight in the choice of the subject matter, but the entire story was re-written and worked on and re-written deliberately. I wanted it to be violent; *it had to be;* I wanted it to really touch people. I wanted it to be shocking. When I sat down to do it I did not know at the time that it would spawn two sequels and one that would take place twenty years down the line. I did not foresee that it would spread itself the way it did. Besides my publisher asking me I have been asked countless times whether this story was not the story of mine that I liked best when it came to all the stuff I have written over the years.

I have to say that all my stories that I write, all the characters that I bring to fictional life, are all my favorites to some degree. Like a parent I feel these are my children. But at the same time I do not feel grieved or annoyed at the preference that some of my readers seem to give to Bobby. It seems that most of my readers adore and fell in love with Bobby. Again, I intended that. I won't say that I fail to understand that. Bobby is a loving, caring, extremely handsome young man that most people would be delighted to have as a partner, so anyone could understand Master Kent's anguish over what befalls his very special "boy" in the opening installment. A friend of mine on the internet who I will simply call "D" told me in no uncertain terms that he absolutely hated the story and in his words, "I threw it away." I felt awful about that of course, but what really surprised me was the base of his dislike. It sounded to me that something similar that happens to Bobby in the story more than likely happened to him as well. I felt bad about that but quickly reminded "D" that the story was not meant to embrace or celebrate what happens to Bobby, rather, to graphically describe and hold back nothing where these matters were concerned. His revelations about the story gave me a lot to think about. Did "D" suffer something like what Bobby did in the story? Did "D" and other people think that I really thought that rape was a joke? I knew that I had to answer these questions strongly and say that *no*, I did not think rape was a joke. The story never says that it is. Such a thing is *wrong*, wrong beyond what I as the author of this story could ever describe. But I can safely assure my readers that the characters in this story are not the product (or products) of cold or perverted thinking. They are not figures of disgust either.

One morning on the train I happened to see two construction

workers, one very young and deliciously handsome, the other older than him and very rugged looking. The way the older construction guy would look at the younger one made me wonder the nature of their relationship. They were both appealing to me for different reasons, which for what I write was as it should have been. They caused the characters of Master Kent and Bobby to be born in my mind and somewhere down the road poor Bobby was unfortunate enough to cross paths with my other two fictional characters, the evil Cleeve and his equally evil cohort, Otis. It is all for me though a form of searching for myself with words that fit the meanings to my life. They are all part of me these characters, and again they are not a part of me. *Christopher Trevor*

Part 1
The Story

Master Kent had heard the stories about Cleeve and Otis. He had even read some of the police report that his good buddy, Police Officer John McLaughlin had permitted him to see one night while he was hanging out with the ruggedly handsome cop at police headquarters in Manhattan. Horrid reports of men being abducted, tortured to nearly within an inch of their lives, worked over real hard, and in all the cases, even raped, brutally raped by the two mysterious men who prowled the city in the wee hours of the morning looking for marks. They seemed to favor a variety of types of men, but even though the men varied in appearance they all shared a common denominator. They were all of the very muscular and physically powerful type. From office executives to construction workers, to cops, to rookie cops, guys in the military and to bodybuilders at the gym, they seemed to go after them all. Officer McLaughlin related a couple of the reports of one cop and one rookie he knew who had on separate occasion's fallen victim to the maniacal Cleeve and his cohort Otis. The cop was still in therapy, two years after his ordeal. It didn't even matter to the two sadistic men if the man they abducted at the time had a wife or children at home. One such married man who demanded anonymity after his capture and eventual release from Cleeve and Otis said that even if the two men were brought to justice he would not testify. What had been done to him was beyond humiliating in his point of view, nothing for his wife, his kid or his peers to know about. With that much in mind the police were able to discern that all the men that Cleeve and Otis had abducted had been released after a while and eventually recovered physically from their awful ordeal, dealt to them by the two appalling kidnappers, but most of them never recovered mentally. The married guy told Officer McLaughlin and another officer how at least twice to three times a week he wakes up in a cold sweat at night. Other men claimed that thoughts and recurring nightmares of being abducted and tortured haunted them on a daily basis. When Master Kent asked his good buddy Officer McLaughlin why no arrests had been made on the two kidnappers the cop explained that in most cases the men who had been abducted had been brought to wherever they were taken blindfolded. Descriptions of Cleeve and Otis were passed around, but thus far no one was able to point them out to the police for arrest purposes. Master Kent, a true and proper leather man of the highest caliber could not believe it, good, honest, hard working innocent men being kidnapped and brutally tortured, it was awful even to think about it. It demoralized the leather master's way of life, seeing as tests of strength and endurance were never torturous, but Cleeve and Otis had made a mockery of it somehow. And the police seemed unable to do much about it. Master Kent huffed miserably and looked at his watch, saw how late it was, and told his cop buddy that he had better be on his way, explaining that his boy would be home soon. He went on to tell Officer McLaughlin that his boy was working late at a job-site that he and his construction crew had been assigned to, racking up on some over-time, but how he wanted to be home when his boy got there. Officer John McLaughlin, an out of the closet police officer told Master Kent how lucky he was to have such a great looking stud for a boy. Master Kent grinned through his salt and pepper colored goatee and said that he agreed totally. The two men shook hands, hugged each other and Master Kent left the police station. When he arrived home and his boy wasn't there the well-built leather man didn't even think to worry, but after two hours went by and his boy still wasn't home he became very concerned. The boy was always punctual and if he needed to be late for whatever the reason he always called his master to let him know. Never however did he think even for a second that his boy could have unwittingly become victim to the psychotic Cleeve and Otis. Never that is until his boy was returned to him very late the next night, beaten nearly to shit and thoroughly exhausted. Robert, known to most of his buddies and to Master Kent as Bobby related in vivid detail exactly all of what he was put through. Master Kent swore revenge on the two men known as Cleeve and Otis. He swore that if it took him the rest of his life *he would* find the two fuckers and make them pay, and pay dearly…

Master Kent, six feet four inches tall with crystal blue eyes, dark crew cut hair with tiny flakes of silver in it and a thick goatee is handsomer than a king and built like a brick shit-house, totally muscular and rock hard from all the working out he does at the gym on a daily basis. At thirty five years of age he is the owner of a hard-core leather bar in Manhattan, the same bar where he met his special boy, Robert

(Bobby), two years ago. Bobby had been hanging out with a few buddies of his and when he and Master Kent saw each other it was like an old fashioned story of love at first sight. Bobby was twenty years old at the time and Master Kent freely admitted that just looking at the guy stole his breath. He sent Bobby a drink and the boy came over to thank him a few minutes later. Master Kent told him that he was the owner of the bar as they shook hands, both of their palms moist with the sweat of passion. The two men got to know each other in ways that only leather men can get to know each other and after six months they were living together. Bobby, the love of Master Kent's life, his pride and joy, now twenty two years old, with buzz-cut light brown hair, piercing dark eyes and no facial hair whatsoever, he is five feet ten inches tall and like Master Kent, totally muscular. But Bobby is not muscular and well-toned from working out at the gym, rather Master Kent's boy is beefy and muscular from the job he works as a construction worker. Master Kent's extraordinary boy slings hammers, carries cinder blocks on his shoulders and totes tools and two by fours all day in all kinds of weather. A real fucking handsome as a prince and devoted muscle boy Master Kent has. Devoted totally and only to his master Bobby shows that devotion in many ways. He licks his master's tired, bare and smelly feet at the end of the long workday; he sucks the sweat out of his master's rancid armpits and licks his master's boots clean. All of this he does with love. All of this is he too happy to do for Master Kent. Every morning Bobby wakes his master by sucking his huge cock, swallows Kent's load and then gulps down his frothy hot piss stream. Bobby never loses a drop of his master's cum or piss. He knows that if he does there will be punishment to endure. Bobby accepts all that Master Kent dotes on him, including the ass paddlings administered to him. The paddling on a daily basis is done with love behind it, never with feelings of anger. The daily ass paddlings remind Bobby of his status to his loving master and at times are also tests of the boy's endurance. The boy's tits are clamped a lot of the time and while he does housework a butt plug is usually wedged tightly in his hole. He is not permitted to shoot his load except at the times when Master Kent grants him permission. Sometimes two weeks or more will go by before Master Kent allows Bobby to shoot his pent-up load. The master loves seeing his boy always on edge, another test of his love and endurance. When Master Kent does finally allow Bobby to relieve himself in a manly way he is only permitted to cum once, which really does little to alleviate the pressure and erotic pain that Bobby's succulent balls are constantly in. Making him shoot that one and only load every couple of weeks keeps the boy anxious and hot to shoot another. It also keeps him very well frustrated and devoted to his master. Bobby's real and truest pleasure is in pleasing Master Kent. The boy's cock is always hard and standing at attention, all nine inches of it. Along with the butt plug that Master Kent keeps wedged in Bobby's hole he also keeps a cock ring fastened tightly around the base of the boy's cock and just above his sexy nut sac. Bobby is not allowed to touch his cock for any reason, except to hold the big guy steady when he pisses. This also reminds the boy that he belongs to Master Kent in body and in mind. Master Kent and his boy Bobby are extremely happy together. Since Bobby moved in with Kent several times the rugged master has suggested (never demanded where this issue is concerned) that the boy quit his job, citing how owning the leather bar makes more than enough money for the two of them to live on comfortably. With the utmost respect Bobby explained how he loved working, how he loved thinking about Master Kent all day while at a job-site and then coming home to him at the end of each day. He also explained how his job as a construction worker kept him in tip-top shape. With all that in mind Master Kent agreed to Bobby's wish to keep working. After that conversation he did however take the boy to the third bedroom of the house, hoisted him into the sling and fucked the tar out of his hole for him, with no lubricant that time, just another test of Bobby's endurance, which he passed with flying colors. The third bedroom in Master Kent's and Bobby's house is actually a dungeon, complete with slings, a real working rack, a long solid oak table equipped with leather straps, and shelves upon shelves of erotically torturous devices. After fucking Bobby hard two times with no lubricant Master Kent had let him out of the sling. The boy knelt before his loving master. With permission Bobby jacked himself off all over Kent's boots and then proceeded to lick all his creamy boy juice off his master's boots, really shining them up for him. Yes, Master Kent and his boy Bobby are tremendously happy together. The way Master Kent sees it Bobby and he will be together for the rest of their lives. Unfortunately, that dream almost changed the night when Bobby never made it home, because that was the night when Kent's poor boy fell victim to those two monsters, Cleeve and Otis...

Bobby had called Kent to tell him that he would be working late at a job-site in Manhattan. He and his crew were working hard renovating the seventh floor in an office building for a company that would be moving in there very soon. Because of the limited amount of time they had to get finished they had agreed to the overtime, citing that the money was not so bad either. Kent told Bobby that it was no problem, and that to kill time he would go visit his good buddy at the police station, adding that he would be home before the boy got there. Before hanging up Bobby said "I love you Master Kent." Kent could feel the smile on the boy's angelic face as he said that and his breath caught in his throat as he told him how much he loved him as well. As the workday finally drew to a close Bobby and his crew were cleaning up the area, putting away their tools, and locking up the workspace. Most of the studly construction crew was wearing shorts, tee shirts or tank tops, hard hats and work boots with sweat socks tucked down in them due to the fact that it was August in New York. The floor they were working on had no air conditioning save for the few small fans they had set up and most of the guys, including Bobby were sweaty and musty smelling, the scents of real young men who had worked hard all day. When it was just Bobby and two of his work buddies left clearing up the area Bobby told the guys to take off, adding that he would finish up the chores and then be on his way as well. One of the guys asked him if he was sure he didn't mind and Bobby said that he did not mind at all. Bobby didn't realize what a fatal mistake that really was. His two buddies left and Bobby was left alone clearing up the worksite. As he was putting some tools away he heard the sound of heavy footsteps from down the hall.

"Hey, you guys still here?" Bobby called out; shucking off his sweat sopped tank top and wiping his huge muscular torso off with it, listening at the same time to the sound of the crunching footsteps. "Hey, who's there?"

As Bobby moved his tank top over his ever-sore nipples a low moan of ecstasy flowed from his lips. The boy's nipples were always sore, because, as mentioned earlier, more often than not Master Kent kept Bobby's cherry sized nubs tightly clamped. When the footsteps halted Bobby tossed his tank top on top of his backpack and listened to the suddenly eerie silence.

"Anybody there?" he called out loudly, his deep voice echoing down the long hallway.

Wearing a pair of faded and ripped denim shorts, his calf length mustard colored work boots, and a pair of moist sweat soaked white sweat socks tucked down in his boots Bobby started walking slowly down the hallway.

"Hello?" he called out again. "Any of you guys still here?"

He stopped walking when he heard the footsteps again, coming from the turn at the end of the hallway. He grinned, trying to mask the feeling of trepidation that was suddenly coursing through him.

"Okay, I know you guys are still here," Bobby said with a sly looking grin on his beguilingly handsome face. "Trying to play a joke on me or something?"

He bravely quickened his pace; his own footsteps crunching on the wood and plaster littered floor. When Bobby turned the corner at the end of the hallway he was surprised to see no one there.

"Shit," he whispered. "What the fuck is going on? Am I hearing things?"

As he turned again and began slowly walking back to the work area he saw that his tank top was no longer atop his backpack where he had tossed it just moments ago. With a look of "What the fuck?" etched on his handsome face Bobby again quickened his pace. Suddenly, the door to the fire exit was thrown open. Two men, both of them dressed in worn jeans; pull over tee shirts with the sleeves cut off them, and heavy-duty work boots rushed madly at Bobby.

"H-hey, who the fuck are you guys?" Bobby asked as the bigger of the two, Cleeve, quickly and meanly grabbed one of the boy's upper muscular arms in a tight vise like grip. "UHHHHFFFFF!!! Hey, fucking let go of me man!!!"

The two guys were huge, epically proportioned. Bobby balled his hands into fists, but before he could do anything Cleeve swung him around bodily and slammed him cruelly against a wall.

"UHHHHNNNFFFFFF!!!" Bobby gasped as his chest and stomach areas connected hard with the brick wall and plaster rained down on him. "WH-*what the fuck???*"

With one huge hand Cleeve grabbed Bobby by the back of his neck, backed him up a few steps and then rammed him again against the wall, totally knocking the wind out of the boy. Then, holding Bobby up by his arm Cleeve pulled him away from the wall and his buddy Otis made one of his huge ham-sized hands into a fist. Otis gave Bobby a hard and packed punch to his stomach.

"OOOOOFFFFF!!!" Bobby grunted and doubled over in searing pain.

Cleeve hauled the boy back up and Otis punched him again in the stomach.

"OOOOFFFF!!!" Bobby grunted again, spittle flying from between his lips, but he could not double over this time as Cleeve held him tightly by his arm.

"WH-what the fuck do you guys want?"Bobby sputtered, more saliva dripping now from his mouth, his lips trembling as he spoke.

"We already have it," Cleeve said mockingly to Kent's boy. "And may I say thank you for being shirtless for us? Saves us the trouble of having to strip you.

Cleeve swing Bobby around again and once more slammed him bodily against the wall...

"AAAARRRHHHH!!!" Bobby cried out awfully. "St-strip me???"

That was when Bobby saw his missing tank top sticking out of the back of one of Cleeve's jeans pockets. Cleeve and Otis then each grabbed one of Bobby's arms and legs and hoisted him seemingly effortlessly up off the floor between them.

"H-hey, what is this???" Bobby stammered in pain and total fear. "P-put me the fuck down you guys!! Put me down now!!"

The two men grinned at each other as they held Bobby aloft and Cleeve said, "Hey Otis, I see a post down at the end of the hall that we can rope this handsome young guy up to" and the two men hoisted their prey higher.

"What say we introduce his balls to that post first?" Cleeve asked his buddy.

The two men dashed down the hallway holding Bobby in the air, his legs spread wide and his big crotch aimed directly at the wooden post they were headed for.

"OHHHRRRR fuck, no, *no!!!*" Bobby ranted and screamed help-lessly, knowing all too well what two men intended to do. "*Ohhhhhhhhhh SHIT, NO!!!*"

When they reached the post they were still moving pretty fast and they slammed poor Bobby's balls into it, hard. His denim shorts took a lot of the blow but his balls still felt as if they had been pulver-ized.

"AAAAARRRRRRRRRR!!!" Bobby screamed in a man's agony and the two men dropped him to the floor in a heap.

The boy lay there with his teeth clenched in agony and his hands placed protectively over his poor wounded balls.

"AAAAAAAAAYYYYYY, GOD," Bobby said in a high-pitched tone of voice. "Wh-why're you two doin' this to me?" In response Cleeve reached down, grabbed the boy under one of his sweaty armpits digging his fingers in real deep, hauled him to his feet, and slammed him up against the post, facing him and Otis.

"YUUUHHHFFFF..." Bobby grunted as he hit the post hard, his balls still searing from the awful blow they had been dealt.

"Otis, get some of that rope we saw him pack away," Cleeve said with authority in his voice. "We can use it to tie this young hot stud to this post.

As muscular and strong as Bobby was he was totally consumed by fear at that moment. He simply looked up at Cleeve in pain and agony. Moments later Bobby's hands were roped tightly behind him and around the post. His strapping upper body was tied up with mounds upon mounds of rope wound over and over his torso, pinning his huge arms to his body. Rope was also tied tightly just under the magnificent young man's big muscular pecs, causing his sore nipples to jut out nice and inviting like for his two sadistic captors. The two men tied Bobby's booted feet to the post in a criss-cross fashion, keeping him totally immobilized. The red sweat soaked bandanna that Bobby kept in his back pocket had been used to blindfold him with. Cleeve and Otis ran their huge mangy hands all over Bobby's body. They squeezed his bowling bowl sized biceps real hard, inflicting pain, they squatted down and gripped his thighs, slapped his stomach area hard and squeezed and teased his sore nipples. They man-handled his aching balls through his shorts. Squeezing Bobby's balls really got a few good wails of pain and utter anguish out of the poor boy.

"Hey Cleeve, his nips look all sore and red for some reason," Otis said as he ran the tips of his big and rough feeling fingers over Bobby's nipples, teasing them and twitching the nubs of them back and forth.

Bobby grimaced miserably behind his blindfold and clenched his teeth.

"Yeah, they sure as fuck do at that," Cleeve mused and twisted one of Bobby's nipples real hard, making the young man scream. "Say guy, what the fuck have you been up to with these big succulent tits of yours eh?"

"M-my, my master, my master keeps my nipples sore for me you bastards!!" Bobby seethed, spittle flying from his mouth. "And I and every part of me belong to him, exclusively!! *So get your stinking paws off me and release me now, if you know what the fuck is good for you!!!"*

"Your master?" Otis asked.

The two men snickered meanly and they each gave Bobby a hard and well packed punch in the stomach.

"OOOOFFFF!!!" Bobby grunted miserably. *"Fucking low life bastards!!"*

"It looks to me like we snagged ourselves some daddies' boy," Cleeve said enthusiastically. "I wonder how the fuck his daddy would feel if he could see his boy now Otis."

When he felt their hands moving over his shorts and unbuttoning them Bobby held his breath in total fear. He knew that they would see the cock ring he was wearing, the cock ring he always wore in honor of the leather master he so loved and adored. They would also see just how hard his huge nine-inch cock was, a real squeeze toy for milking like crazy Bobby's cock was.

"NO, NO, oh God no," Bobby panted angrily, trying desperately to get himself untied, every muscle in his huge arms flexing involuntarily under the tight binding ropes. "L-leave my damned shorts on me you bastards!!"

Ignoring him they ripped Bobby's shorts from him. His cock stood straight up, stalked up thick and hard and succulent looking, pointing at the ceiling. His wounded balls hung down low and tight with the cock ring snapped around the base of them. Pre cum and beads of piss slithered from the boy's cock slit.

"When the fuck was the last time you shot your load boy?" Cleeve asked Bobby, addressing him as his master would have while running the tips of his fingers over the crown of Bobby's rock hard cock. "I would bet your master is one of those fuckers who don't let you get off unless he says so. This fucking meat stick of yours looks like its ready to spew a load right the fuck now boy. And what a gargantuan size it is, eh Otis?"

"Well said man, even for such a sadistic fucker such as you," Bobby seethed angrily. "And I love my master for it, now untie me and..."

But Bobby's words were cut short as Otis clamped his mouth down hard on one of Bobby's sore nipples and at the same time Cleeve began slowly stroking his big meat stick. Cleeve used the boy's pre cum as a lube to make his cock good and slick. Bobby swore like a captured marine saying, "OOOHHRRRRR no, no, n-not this you slimy fuckers!! Get your fucking mangy paws off me; get your paws off me *now!!! OH SHIT, you two are goin' to make me shoot my damned load here!!!*"

It didn't take all that long for Bobby to cum and shoot that first very pent-up load for the sadistic Cleeve and Otis as he had almost a three week supply of his good stuff stored up in his big beautiful balls. As Cleeve stroked him more and more and Otis licked, sucked and slurped at his nipple Bobby let loose with what seemed like endless ropes of creamy thick spunk.

"AAAAARRRRHHHHH FUCK!!!" Bobby panted in utter and helpless ecstasy. "Got me fucking creaming like a real bitch in heat!!"

What Cleeve and Otis didn't know was just how much Bobby could take. What they had dished out on him was nothing...yet... Cleeve stroked the boy and Otis stopped slurping at his nip to watch and stare in awe as Bobby shot long rope after long rope of his creamy jazz.

"God alfuckingmighty Cleeve, the fuckin' kid has a ton of the juice in him it looks like," Otis exclaimed, his fingers on one of Bobby's jutted up nips.

"OOHHHRRRRR GAWD," Bobby roared like a lion as his cum was siphoned from him and landed all over the floor in big soupy globs.

When he was (finally) done Cleeve and Otis each leaned down and meanly slurped one of Bobby's nipples each into their greedy mouths.

"AAAAARRRR NO, no you fuckers!!" Bobby gasped. "Don't fuckin' suck my poor nips so soon after I've gotten off!! My tits're so fucking sensitive after I've shot a big creamy load!!"

In response Bobby felt a hand close tight around his now semi hard cock and begin stroking him all over again.

"OHHHHHHRRRR NO, no, now this is too much you bastards!!" Bobby ranted and his eyes crossed behind his blindfold as his head spun.

In what seemed like nearly no time at all the boy shot another hefty sized load of ball juice all over the floor as whoever had his cock in hand stroked the fuck out of it. Bobby could see in his mind's eye as his huge slit spewed forth his sexy mess as he again swore like a military man.

"AAAAAAARRRR SHIT, lookit me cummin' a second fucking time!!" Bobby panted breathlessly, the back of his head pressed against the post he was trussed to.

The two men went on meanly sucking, licking and even bighting hard on Bobby's nips after he was done shooting that second load of cream for them.

"AAARRRRRR GOD, my poor fucking nips!" Bobby swore miserably as his muscular body broke out in a sweat and glistened in the heat.

He felt their hands squeezing his tight balls and pulling on the hairs on his nut sac. When they pulled a few hairs out of his sac Bobby screamed in a real man's agony. Cleeve and Otis continued slurping madly at the boy's nipples, really putting the screws to them, squeezing his pulsing balls and stroking his hyper sensitive to the touch cock as well.

"You fuckers," Bobby gasped. "My master will get you for this!!"

"Maybe he will boy, maybe he will get us, but he sure as fuck ain't going to be getting you for a while," Cleeve said menacingly, taking his mouth off the nipple he had been working on.

Bobby's jaw dropped at the sound of those words and his softening cock twitched in fear... He asked just what the fuck that was supposed to mean as he again felt a huge hand encircle his big cock.

"It means, you beautiful fucking piece of ass," Cleeve said as he meanly yanked Bobby's sensitive feeling cock. "...that you're going to be taking a ride, a long fucking ride with us to my house for some real fun...and when you find out what my meaning of fun is you will never be the same boy..."

"G-God no," Bobby panted, in a total and blinding panic now at the thought of being kidnapped. "PL-please g-guys..."

But his words were cut off again as Cleeve squeezed his cock super hard.

"OHHHRRR SHIT, easy with my poor cock you bastard!!" Bobby reeled as Cleeve twisted his cock around.

When the boy felt the tip of a finger jammed into his cock slit he nearly flew out of his work boots. Instead he pissed long and frothy on the floor, his stream mixing with the mess of his cum down there.

"Shit man, when his work buddies show up here tomorrow

morning and find this mess of cum and piss all over the floor they're going to think that six or seven guys jacked off here," Otis said, taking his mouth off Bobby's other nipple. "No one would ever think that just one hot boy got his cock milked and pissed like crazy."

"Yeah, and we ain't leaving him here for them to find either so he can tell them all about it either," Cleeve said, squatting down and rummaging through Bobby's backpack. "Not like that other construction worker we practically ate the plump nips off of, Paul his name was, Paul's nipples were mighty tasty!" **(The story "Paul's Nipples" starred Cleeve and Otis and was printed in MACH magazine, issue # 41.)**

Cleeve found the prize he sought in Bobby's backpack. Smiling evilly, he held up a pair of sharp teethed tit clamps.

"Tell me something boy, do you always carry tit clamps with you in your pack?" Cleeve asked Bobby.

"I keep them with me per my master's instructions," Bobby spat. "But a lowlife like you wouldn't understand that..."

Cleeve smiled again and said, "Okay Otis, lets get this boy ready and packaged for the ride to my house!" With that Cleeve snickered, stood up and clipped the tit clamps onto Bobby's overly tender and sore nipples. The boy screamed in total pain, his shrill voice echoing through the long hallway and work area as he pleaded for the men to take the clamps off his nipples.

"Better gag him Otis my man," Cleeve said.

The next thing Bobby knew a foul smelling and awful tasting cloth was being crammed into his mouth. He guessed it to be an old ratty sock of one of the two men who had captured him.

"RRRMMMMMFFFFF!!!" Bobby sputtered madly as a rope was then tied over the foul smelling sock in his mouth, jamming it tightly in there.

"Okay Otis, looks like he's ready to go," Cleeve said delightedly.

They untied Bobby from the post, quickly re-tied his hands behind him at the wrists as he struggled fruitlessly, left his upper body and feet tied, and loaded the terrified boy into a wooden crate.

"Say Cleeve, he's blindfolded, why put him in a crate too?" Otis asked.

"Why not?" Cleeve asked and slammed the lid shut atop the crate.

The two men laughed fiendishly…

Dressed as construction workers, and being that there was construction going on in the building no one bothered to question the two men as they wheeled the huge crate out of the office building on a dolly, not even Carmine, the nightshift security guard on duty at the front desk. Outside, behind the building was where Cleeve had parked their van. They loaded the crate containing Bobby into the back section of the van, slammed the doors closed and walked to the front section of the vehicle.

"Do you think its okay to leave the kid cooped up in that crate for the entire ride?" Otis asked Cleeve.

"Sure, it has two air holes cut into the side of it," Cleeve responded and the two men climbed up into the van, Cleeve settling into the driver's seat.

As the van began moving Bobby's heart pounded with total fear. Sweat dripped off him everywhere and he cried big tears behind his blindfold as he thought of Master Kent…

The boy estimated that the ride took a little more than two hours; nearly three hours actually that Cleeve and Otis kept him in that crate. When they arrived at Cleeve's upstate house they opened the back doors of the van, hopped inside, and yanked the top of the crate open. Master Kent's boy was practically unconscious in there and dripping with sweat, and then, shaking like a leaf in a hurricane as they hoisted him out and to his tied feet. Bobby's nipples were further than swollen at that point and the two men had to help him keep his balance as he tottered there. His cock was shriveled and soft as it hung over his balls, all slimy looking from the way it had been stroked and milked earlier.

"Hey boy, you all right there?" Cleeve asked and took the blindfold off him.

Bobby let his eyes adjust to the lamppost light in front of the huge sprawling house, all alone and by itself, surrounded by nothing but dense woods and the road in front of it. The area was totally deserted. It was outright desolate. As his head cleared a bit Master Kent's boy looked at the two men questioningly; fear and wonder mixed in his look.

"Mmmmfffff?" he said helplessly.

"Welcome to my home," Cleeve said and undid the rope around

the gag in the boy's mouth before taking the rancid sock out.

"Wh-where the fucks have you brought me?" Bobby asked the two men. "What is this fucking place?"

"It ain't no vacation spot for you that's for sure boy," Cleeve said and rapped Bobby hard across his firm butt cheeks.

"OWWWWW!!!" Bobby growled, standing there on his tied feet, turning his head from side to side, taking in his surroundings in awe.

Cleeve pushed Bobby to the opened doors of the van on his tied feet and then meanly and unceremoniously pushed him out of the vehicle and to the pavement.

"UUUHHFFFFFF!!!" Bobby grunted as he hit the ground all tied up, no way to break his fall.

The boy quickly turned on his back and looked up at Cleeve and Otis as they stepped down out of the van.

"What a shitty thing to do to a poor guy!!" Bobby panted as he struggled to get himself to his feet before Cleeve could again put his hands on him, still taking in the sight of the sprawling huge house in front of him in the lamppost light.

The boy managed to get himself into a squatting position and then got himself standing on his tied up booted feet. He wondered who the fuck Cleeve was that he owned all this, desperately curious as to how the man could have attained such wealth. (Actually, all of the men before him who had been captured and brought to Cleeve's house were amazed by it and wondered just whom the fuck Cleeve was that he could afford such an immense and impressive place.) Bobby's thoughts were cut short when Cleeve yanked hard on the thin chain connected to the boy's tit clamps.

"YOWWWWW!!!" Bobby roared, practically losing his balance on his tied feet. "Fucker..."

"Still think that that master of yours will find you here boy?" Cleeve asked Bobby mockingly.

Bobby looked around again and again and gulped hard, knowing that rescue was very far away, if at all. Cleeve took the tit clamps off Bobby's nipples, slammed the boy up against the van, and he and Otis leaned down, and again slurped one of his nipples each into their mouths.

"AAARRRRR!!!" Bobby screamed into the dark night as the blood rushed madly back into his overworked and overly tortured nipples as the two men feasted and bit wildly on them.

"Fuckers..." Bobby squeaked.

A short while later the two men slung Bobby across their big broad shoulders and carried him still tied up into the big stately looking house... Bobby swore like a captured marine, demanding to be released as the two men carried him into the house, his cock swaying in the wind...

A Few Hours Later

Needless to say Master Kent did not sleep a wink that night. At two AM he called his cop buddy, Officer John McLaughlin, who was still on duty at the police station pulling a double shift. The cop's private office number rang and he answered the phone on the second ring. When Master Kent told him that his boy had never arrived home that night the cop instantly recalled the leather master telling him that the kid had worked late at a construction job-site. Officer McLaughlin then said three words that sent a chill up Master Kent's spine, "Cleeve and Otis." The cop assured Master Kent that his boy would turn up though, adding that he would put out word to his officers out there to be on the lookout for him. And, to also be on the lookout for a van that looked like the one those other men had reported being abducted in by Cleeve and Otis. Unfortunately though Bobby was already long gone from the city and so was the van. Officer McLaughlin knew this sad fact, based on the past stories he had heard of the two men known only as Cleeve and Otis, how after capturing their prey they always hightailed it out of the city to a very far away and unknown destination. Master Kent's cop buddy however reassured the leather man again, trying to somehow pacify him, but in his heart Master Kent knew that his poor boy faced horrible danger at the hands of those two crazed men. Trying to think of anywhere else his boy might be, knowing there was nowhere he thanked his cop buddy and put the phone down with a trembling hand. He thought helplessly about Bobby being in the clutches of those two maniacs and a feeling of desperation filled him while he wondered what those bastards were doing to his poor boy.

After carrying Bobby into the house a few hours earlier they had slammed him down on his stomach on a long oak table in a huge main floor room of the vast house. The poor boy squirmed miserably atop the table as Otis untied his feet and spread his legs apart by his ankles, pulling him halfway off the table. They tied Bobby's booted feet to the legs of the table, keeping his legs spread wide and exposing his pink and very gaping rosebud of an asshole.

"Damn, damn, DOUBLE damn, just as I thought, a real sweet, tight looking pussy hole," Cleeve commented fiendishly and jammed a big thumb into Bobby's hole.

"AAAYYYRRRR GAWD," Robert grunted, turning and looking at Cleeve angrily. "FUCKER, get your damned thumb out of my hole man!!"

"Heh, heh, boy, that should be all we're going to jam in that great looking shit chute of yours," Cleeve said, yanked his thumb out of Bobby's hole, and the poor terrified kid gulped loudly in fear. "Otis, would you please begin?"

Fear filled Bobby's eyes as Otis picked up a black leather case from under the table. He opened it and displayed the various sized dildos that were in it.

"OHHHHH no, no," Bobby wailed pitifully atop the table and squirmed in the bondage. "My master will kill you both for this shit!!"

"He'll have to find us first you gorgeous stud," Cleeve said.

Cleeve then spit twice into Bobby's hole and prodded it deeply with two fingers, truly digging those fingers in as if he were searching for gold. Bobby seethed and swore as Cleeve primed him for a massive fuck session. Otis chose the smallest of the dildos and placed a tray of ice cubes on the table next to Bobby as Cleeve pulled his fingers out of the boy's hole, spit into it again, and really moistened it up. Otis jammed the dildo into Bobby's mouth, meanly forcing him to suck it like it was a cock.

"Yeah, that's it boy, get that thing all wet," Otis said meanly. "Dribble on it boy, get it super wet because where it's going you'll need it to be more than wet. You'll need it to be saturated."

"RRRRMMMMMFFFF..." Bobby sputtered miserably and dribbled gobs of saliva onto the latex device, sucking at it like crazy as Otis fucked his mouth with it.

Cleeve spit two more times into Bobby's hole and then took an ice cube from the tray laying next to the tied up boy on the table. He rubbed the freezing square cube against Bobby's pink moistened hole and Bobby grunted in agony around the dildo being thrust in and out of his mouth. Cold chills crept up Bobby's muscular spine and he shivered uncontrollably as Cleeve rubbed and rubbed the melting ice cube against the walls of his hole. When the cube was small enough Cleeve slipped it into the kid's hole and watched it disappear deep inside him. Cleeve cackled as he said it looked like Bobby's hole ate the ice cube, literally sucked it in.

"GGGRRRRFFFFF!!!" Bobby wailed madly as the ice cube invaded his poor hole and Otis jammed the dildo still further into his mouth, practically making him deep throat the damned thing, choking the poor boy with it. "RRRRRMMMFFFFFFFF!!!!"

Smiling fiendishly Cleeve took another ice cube from the tray and began rubbing it against the boy's hole. Bobby squirmed in total agony now on the table and he was having trouble breathing as Otis forced the dildo further into his craw. Saliva spewed out of the sides of Bobby's mouth around the dildo that was at that point wetly saturated and totally lubricated with his warm saliva. Otis took it slowly from the boy's mouth and held it up.

"Looks like its ready to be introduced to the kid's hole," Otis said gleefully to Cleeve.

"OH GOD NO, NO," Robert gasped, tears filling his beautiful eyes, looking up in fear at the dildo and then looking beseeching at Otis. "Please man; don't do this to me…"

Cleeve smiled and forced the still big ice cube into Bobby's asshole.

"AAAYYYYRRRR," Bobby grunted as his cock swung out from under him and pointed at the floor, chock filled with piss and (fear) hard as a rock.

His balls, still cock ringed jutted out tight and hard above the boy's superb looking meat stick.

"Oh Good God, no," Bobby roared then as Otis handed the saliva lubed dildo to Cleeve. "My hole belongs only to my master… Oh God, you fuckers…"

Cleeve pressed the tip of the dildo against Bobby's moist hole. The boy's hole having been moistened up did little to ease the pain as the dildo was slowly wedged in there.

"AAAARRRGGHH, you fucking, fucking lowlife bastards!!" Bobby growled as tears of seething anger flowed from his eyes.

Cleeve pushed the dildo in further and rotated it as it went, driving the boy crazy, making him dizzy.

"And just think Otis, this is the smallest dildo that was in that case," Cleeve snickered.

"OHHHRRRR shit, shit," Bobby gasped throatily and his hard cock bobbed back and forth under him.

He desperately held his piss in check as Cleeve slipped the dildo still further into his hole, stretching that hole as the boy howled loud and in pain.

"Holy crow Otis, just look at how this sweet boy's hole is eating up this damn dildo," Cleeve laughed and pushed the latex device still deeper inside Bobby's aching hole.

At that point the device was just about halfway in Bobby's hole. Thoughts of when Master Kent tested him in this fashion filled his mind. But when his master tested him in this way it wasn't done to torture him, rather it was done with love and understanding along with the tests of pain and endurance. Also, Master Kent never used such a gargantuan device on his boy's hole. Bobby clenched his teeth and cried pitifully as he thought of his loving master. Cleeve rotated the dildo some more as he pushed it in till only a very small amount of it was showing from Bobby's hole. Cleeve let go of the device and ordered the boy to squeeze his luscious looking ass cheeks tightly together around the invasive atrocity in his shit chute, giving one of the boy's ass cheeks a hard and resounding slap to enforce his words. Bobby narrowed his eyes in pain and with no other choice in the matter did as he was told, holding the dildo tightly wedged in his most private channel.

"Look at that Otis, a very well trained boy if ever there was one," Cleeve said and hunkered down at Bobby's hard pulsing cock.

Otis squatted next to Cleeve and the two men began licking and slurping at Bobby's big cock ringed balls, running their tongues over the inside shaft of his rock hardness, sending shivers and chills up the boy's spine.

"OOOOOOhhhhh, God," Bobby whispered, curled his bound hands into one big fist and sweating like a pig held his ass cheeks tight around the dildo in his hole as it tortured the fuck out of him. "Fucking kidnappers…perverts…"

Then, Bobby's head snapped up and his eyes filled with shock as he felt a pair of lips close around his meat stick and begin sucking him. As his big cock was sucked by Otis Cleeve stood and grabbed the end of the dildo. He thrust the big thing in and out of the boy's hole, fucking him with it like a madman as Otis sucked his manhood.

"OHHHHRRRR SHIT," Bobby panted and lifted his head up higher off the table. "Goin' to make me shoot my damned load again

"Damn Cleeve, by the time we fuck him his hole is going to be beyond primed," Otis said meanly.

The two men laughed sadistically as Bobby lay there in pain and agony... Cleeve twisted the second dildo around in the boy's asshole. The second dildo tormented the sides of Bobby's inner sanctum to no end and with his teeth clenched in anger he seethed awfully as Cleeve pushed and twisted the dildo further yet into his already stretched crevice.

Fucking bastards," Bobby spat at his two captors. "Fuckers, planning to keep me here till tomorrow huh??? You guys better kill me then, because my master will spend the rest of his life hunting your sorry asses down!!"

The two men looked at each other across the table that Bobby was sprawled on and they smiled fiendishly at each other. Then, Cleeve picked up a third dildo and tossed it to Otis.

"Your turn Otis my man," Cleeve said and yanked the second rough edged dildo out of Bobby's wounded hole.

"Oh no, no man, please, not with that one too!!" Bobby pleaded when he saw the size of the third dildo and Otis stepped behind him. "OHHHHHH GODS, *please you guys...please...*"

The third dildo made the first two pale in comparison when it came to size and girth. As Otis began pushing the monstrous device into the boy's hole Bobby slammed his head down on the table and screamed and was racked with sobs of pain as his hole was stretched and fucked a third time. Cleeve slapped the boy's tight ass buns hard as Otis pushed and twisted the dildo further and further into his poor hole. When the dildo was all the way in his hole Bobby's head spun as Cleeve took a turn sucking his flaccid cock. By now the poor kid's cock was sore and aching as well from having been overly sucked and made to shoot a few loads. His whimpers and sobs of pain and agony didn't stop Cleeve though from abusing his cock some more as Otis thrust the dildo in and out of his hole. In fact, Bobby's sobs and screams only seemed to spur the two men on all the more.

"OHHHRRRRR SHIT, shit," the boy croaked as Cleeve swirled his tongue greedily over the sensitive crown of Bobby's slimed up cock. "This is sick fucking torture you guys!!"

A while later the third dildo was out of Bobby's hole and Otis was giving him a cool drink of water through a straw. The captive boy sipped the water gratefully, as Cleeve thrust his huge monster-sized cock in and out of his stretched and aching hole.

"Damn Cleeve, just how much do you suppose this tough boy can take?" Otis asked his buddy, his own big hard cock sticking perversely out of his jeans, long, hard, fat, pulsing and hungry to be poked into Bobby's rosebud of a hole. "After having worked his shit chute with those dildos and those ice cubes how many times do you think we should fuck him?"

"Till we're fucking spent and then some more," Cleeve grunted and slapped the boy's butt super hard.

"OWWWWRRRR!!!" Bobby gasped.

Cleeve shot a mean, man-sized load into Bobby's hole, flooding the kid thoroughly with his hot sticky juices.

"OHHHHH yeah," Cleeve grunted breathlessly, slapping Bobby's firm sexy butt cheeks over and over, reddening them now as he seemed to cum and cum like crazy. "Fucking hot boy you are." Cleeve's cock slipped out of Bobby's hole and Otis wasted no time whatsoever. He quickly stepped behind the boy's spread legs and rammed his big fat cock into Bobby's tender asshole.

"AAAYYYYYRRR MY GOD," Bobby grunted and his eyes crossed.

All totaled the two men fucked Bobby long and hard three times each and then just to hear him cry some more they rammed him again with the three dildos. By the time they were done it was two AM the same time that Master Kent was at home wondering just what was happening to his poor boy. And at that point Bobby was just about unconscious. His hole had been stretched beyond reason and it was saturated with globs upon globs of the two men's cum. They untied his booted feet from the legs of the table, leaving his arms tied up behind him and his upper body roped tight. Cleeve lifted the boy off the table like a bridegroom carrying his bride over the threshold of their honeymoon suite.

"I'll put this boy to bed for the night," Cleeve said, carrying Bobby toward a door and then down a long flight of stairs.

"Time for beddy-bye beautiful boy?" Cleeve whispered in Bobby's ear as he lugged him down the stairs and pecked him on the cheek.

He strapped Bobby down to a table in the basement of the house that had been remodeled into a dungeon of sorts. Laying there on his back, strapped down tight Bobby looked around the basement/dungeon through hazy vision. He saw shelves upon shelves on which were an assortment of torturous looking devices. These devices included dildos (his asshole twitched as he took in the sight of the dildos) of many sizes and textures, handcuffs, leather hoods, blindfolds, gags, mean looking butt plugs, and an array of many other things such as whips, paddles, floggers and cat o' nine tails hanging on pegs along the wall. In the center of the basement/dungeon was an old fashioned but very new and working rack, almost like the one that Master Kent had in his basement Bobby thought. As the boy thought of Master Kent his tears flowed and he trembled under the straps...

Bobby slept fitfully through the night, his cock ringed manhood semi hard and slumped over his big aching balls...

The Next Morning

Bobby really hadn't slept much that night, mainly due to the position he was in (Master Kent never made his boy sleep in restraints, not even to punish him) and the pain his poor hole was feeling. Otis leaning down over him on the table that he was still strapped to awakened him as the guy was sucking his morning erection and squeezing his juicy balls. Bobby slowly opened his eyes, praying that it had all been a horrible nightmare and that he would awaken to find that it was Master Kent waking him by sucking his cock.

"OOOOOOOOOOhhhhhh shit, sucking me off first thing in the morning huh man?" Bobby croaked through a scratchy throat and sounded disappointed when he saw it was Otis with his cock in his mouth. "Fucking sick kidnappers can't seem to leave my damned cock alone!! SHIT man, suckin' me off like crazy you are..."

The boy managed to lift his head up off the table and look down at Otis as he sucked his big meat.

"Fucker, you and your friend are going to pay for all of this," Bobby whispered angrily and lay his head back down, looking up at the ceiling. "My master will find the two of you, and when he does you'll both regret ever having snagged my ass! UHHHHHHHH, suckin' me real heavy now you bastard... And more than that you'll regret having fucked my ass! That's my master's domain you sick fuck! OH GAWD MAN, you're goin' to have me creaming any second now fucker."

The boy shot a load like gangbusters, grunting, groaning and squirming under the binding straps as Otis gulped down his morning load.

"OHHHHRRRR GOD," Bobby gasped. "Fucker, seems like this is the least you can do for me after all."

When Bobby was done shooting his load Otis stood up over him.

"You're going to eat a light breakfast boy," Otis said harshly, the remnants of Bobby's cum dripping from his lips, a twisted sight if ever the boy saw one. "Then my buddy and I are taking you out into the woods for a nice nature hike. Doesn't that sound just great you gorgeous fuck?"

Bobby squirmed miserably atop the table as Otis squeezed the tip of his sensitive cock real hard, getting a loud gasp out of him.

After a very quick breakfast of cold cereal and water (no gourmet foods like Master Kent had gotten his boy used to) Bobby found himself stripped of his work boots and sweat socks and standing outside the big house, standing between Cleeve and Otis. The two men had stripped the boy totally naked at that point. His muscular and aching arms were *still* tied tightly up behind him, the tit clamps were on his nipples again and torturing them horribly and his cock and balls were still cock ringed and feeling awful since the day before. He stood between his two captors with his head hanging down, dripping and stinking of sweat, his cock piss hard in front of him and pointing straight out. Cleeve and Otis hadn't allowed Bobby to use the bathroom so he could piss. The boy was totally consumed with fear and was terror stricken beyond reason. It was at least ninety degrees that day along with one hundred percent humidity and the boy was in no condition for what he was about to endure. Cleeve and Otis were appropriately dressed in hiking shorts, hiking boots, and tee shirts. Cleeve slung a backpack filled with supplies over the boy's back.

"Ah, nothing like a day out in the woods to commune with nature, eh boy?" Cleeve asked Bobby mockingly and gave one of his delectable butt cheeks a hard squeeze, practically hoisting him off the ground.

"Fucker, I'm not ready for a damned walk in the woods," Bobby seethed, his head still hanging down.

"Well, ready or not boy we're ready, and you are going," Cleeve said meanly.

That said Cleeve grabbed a long wooden rake pole that was leaning up against the house. It had what was left of old metal rake tines on the end of it. He wedged it between Bobby's legs and up against his cock ringed balls. He instructed Otis to get some rope out of the pack on Bobby's back and they tied the end of the long pole to Bobby's aching balls. Looking down Bobby's jaw dropped in terror as he saw what they were doing. Then, with the other end of the pole in hand Cleeve began pushing the boy forward toward the hot and dense woods on his bare feet.

"RRRRRRHHHHHHHHHH…OH MY GOD!!!" Bobby seethed as he was plodded along and his balls were tortured awfully.

A few times Cleeve pulled on the pole, yanking Bobby's balls up and under his ass crack, Cleeve laughing and saying what a pretty sight that was, the kids balls tucked nice and tight under his ass crack of all places.

"Say Cleeve, I want a turn driving him too," Otis said merrily.

"You'll get your turn soon Otis my man," Cleeve responded. "I'm having way too much fun at the moment.

The two men laughed harshly and meanly as the boy stumbled along with that pole tied to his balls. The small metal rake tines rubbed against Bobby's skin, irritating him like crazy. He stumbled and hobbled along with his head hanging down and dripping sweat. His bare feet were muddied, scratched and scraped up in less than ten minutes of walking. Thorn bushes grated his poor calves and scratched harshly at them. Mosquitoes, flies and other insects found their way to him and nipped and bit him. Bobby had all to do just to stay on his poor bare feet as the two men pushed him along deeper and deeper into the woods.

"F-fuckers, this is a rotten way to treat a guy," Bobby gasped and plodded along faster when Cleeve pushed him hard with the pole bound to his swelling balls.

"Less bullshit talk and more walk boy!!" Cleeve yelled at him and Otis threw a small rock at Bobby's butt cheeks at nearly sixty miles per hour.

"YOWWWWWWWW!!!" Bobby screamed as Otis tossed a second rock at his butt cheeks, equally as speedy, almost like a professional baseball pitcher would, the pain stinging and burning the boy's ass cheek all at once. "OHHHHHRRRRR YOU bastards!!!"

Otis then found a splintery piece of fallen tree branch. He trotted up behind the boy and began whacking Bobby's butt cheeks hard with the branch.

"YAHHHRRRRRR!!!" Bobby bellowed, his voice echoing through the hot woods.

"Come on kid, mush, move along there!" Otis tauntingly said to Bobby and whacked his butt cheeks again and again with the tree branch.

Bobby heaved his huge chest forward and moved along...

"Well Cleeve, if you're not going to let me drive him with the pole I'll drive him with this tree branch..." Otis laughed.

Large tears welled in the boy's eyes and slid down his beautiful face...

When they came to a very large oak tree they had been walking nearly a half-hour. For Bobby though it felt more like two to three hours. His balls were swollen to the most unusual proportions, his clamped nipples were the size of two big freaky looking bullets on his muscular chest, his butt cheeks were a horrid mess of red scratches and big welts, and his feet were more than a total mess. Cleeve had force walked him through mud puddles and at one point he had made the barefoot boy walk over rocks. As Bobby struggled awfully, crying while walking on the rocks Cleeve tugged hard on the pole lashed to the kid's nuts and said "Whoa there boy, time for a breather." Bobby stopped, climbed carefully down off the rocks and stood there again with his head hanging down, gasping, crying loudly and stinking with sweat. Cleeve let the pole fall to the ground and it tugged hard on the boy's poor balls, jarring them unmercifully.

"AAAYYYRRR..." Robert screamed looking down at his aching semi shriveled up cock.

Cleeve and Otis each took canteens of water off their belts. The two men swigged their water and Bobby looked at them desperately. Snickering, they each gave the boy a hearty drink each from their canteens.

"There you go boy, drink up, you really look like you need it bad," Cleeve said, holding the canteen to the boy's trembling lips with this other big hand placed on the back of Bobby's head. "Just because you're having the tar whipped outa you don't mean you should die of thirst."

"Th-thank you, thank you," Bobby whispered when he was done drinking.

Smiling, the two men hooked their canteens back to their belts. Judging from the way they were smiling Bobby knew he was in for more nastiness. Cleeve untied the pole from the boy's balls, took the backpack off his back, and pushed him up against the large oak tree. Cleeve opened the backpack and took out some rope. Tossing some of the rope to Otis he said, "Let's get busy." Within a few minutes Bobby was tightly lashed to the big tree, rope wound tightly around him from his upper body down to his ankles.

"So boy, enjoying the walk so far?" Cleeve asked Bobby and rubbed the tip of a finger over the very tip of one of Bobby's bullet sized clamped nipples.

"Y-yeah, just great," Bobby replied softly and sarcastically. "Just what I've always wanted to do, walk buck naked through the unforgiving woods..."

"Watch your mouth boy, I did you a solid taking that pole off your balls," Cleeve said meanly. "Keep talking like that and I'll hook it back up again when we start walking again."

"Shit," Bobby whispered.

Then, Cleeve and Otis stood at the boy's sides and looking hungrily at his poor clamped nipples they took the tit clamps off him.

"AAAAAYYYYRRRRRR!!!!!" Bobby roared in tortured and twisted agony as the blood rushed furiously back into his poor nipples.

The two men leaned down and they each slurped one of the boy's nipples into their mouths...

"AAAYYYYRRRR SHIT, no, no, you fuckers!!" Bobby gasped, cried and squirmed helplessly under the ropes binding him to the tree. "OH FUCK man, my poor tits are more than fucking sensitive, having been clamped for so damned long!! PLEASE..."

Ignoring him and loving his ranting at the same time the two men slurped, licked, and sucked heartily at the boy's over-sized and aching nipples. His cock grew hard between his legs and stalked straight up, much to his disbelief, oozing pre cum and beads upon beads of piss. Cleeve hooked a hand around Bobby's cock and slowly stroked him as he and Otis went on eating the fuck out of his nipples.

"AAARRRHHHH GODS, *fuckers*," Bobby panted in a high pitched tone of voice. "Fucking bastards just can't get enough of my damned nips and torturing the fuck out of my cock!"

It took a while because of the awful and maddening pain he was in but Bobby spewed a hearty mess of ball juice all over the ground in front of him.

"AAAAAYYYYRRRRRR, got me cummin' and steaming again you

fuck!!" Bobby gasped, wishing they would stop slurping his nipples at that point.

No such luck for the boy though. After Bobby was spent spewing his load his nipples (like most men's out there) became even more sensitive to the touch and the two men took full advantage of that fact. They slurped harder and harder at them, really sucking the fuck out of them. Bobby screamed loudly through a very scratchy throat. When he thought he would go totally and completely crazy Cleeve and Otis stopped eating his nipples. Bobby stood there bound to the tree, breathing unevenly, his cock hanging down, shriveled again and pulsing numbly, filled with piss. Unable to hold it any longer the boy pissed a long yellow stream all over his fucked up feet.

"AAAAYYYRRRRRRR!!!" Bobby screamed again as the piss burned his cut up feet.

"Oh man, that's bad boy, real fucking bad," Cleeve said, nodding his head from side to side.

"What the fuck do you mean?" Bobby asked him angrily.

"Pissing without our permission is a severe offense," Cleeve explained. "Didn't your master teach you any better?"

"My master taught me more than well," Bobby spat. "And I'll piss when the fuck I need to and when the fuck I want! You two bastards are not my masters, not by a long shot!! Its guys like you that give a bad name to loving masters like mine! And furthermore, I do not take orders from lowlife kidnappers such as yourselves!!"

Bobby felt a sense of elation speed through him at having told the two men off, but to his dismay he was still their prisoner. And if they planned on punishing him for pissing without permission he shuddered to think what he would be in for, for shooting off his mouth as he had just done.

Otis then squatted down at the backpack, reached into it, and brought out two round black leather paddles. He tossed one to Cleeve and the two men got busy real quick, paddling and mashing the boy's jutted up and sore nipples real hard.

"AAAAHHRRRRRRRR!!!!" Bobby screamed anew, tears again streaming down his cheeks as the two men paddled his nipples and beat his huge pecs to a crimson tint at the same time. "SHIT, SHIT, you fucking guys!!"

"We'll see who you take orders from boy," Cleeve said through clenched teeth and rapped one of Bobby's nipples super hard with his leather paddle.

The sound of the paddle connecting with his nipples and pecs was maddening to the poor kid...

When Bobby's nipples were mashed down and his pecs were beyond crimson his two captors stopped beating on them, leaned down, and again slurped the boy's nipples back into their mouths.

"AAAYYYYRRRR SHIT, having another go at my poor tits huh you fuckers?" Bobby gasped through clenched teeth.

They sucked Bobby's nipples back up again and then began beating at them all over again with their leather paddles, rapping his huge pecs again as well just for the fuck of it. Bobby grimaced miserably, clenched his teeth again and sobbed loudly and like crazy as the two men brutally beat the tar out of his nipples and pecs.

"So tell me boy, you about ready to take orders from us?" Cleeve asked and whacked, whacked, whacked the kid's nipples with brute force with his leather paddle. "Think that next time you need to piss you'll ask our permission first??? HUH boy???"

"F-fuck you..." Robert stammered as spittle flew from his mouth.

When the tips of Bobby's nipples were mashed down again the two men once more slurped them back up again, really suckling and tonguing at the tender nubs. And then, when the boy's nipples were overly erect they snapped the tit clamps back onto them, a horrible thing to do to them after all the tortures they'd just endured. If Bobby hadn't been tied to the tree he would have fallen to his knees in agony and pain.

"*Y-you fucking bastards, you sick fucks,*" Bobby snuffed and sniveled as his nipples stung and felt like they were on fire on his chest.

"Good job Otis," Cleeve said, handing his paddle to his buddy. "His tits look real sore and ripe. I think we deserve a reward for a job so well done."

"Could not agree with you more," Otis said and put the leather paddles back into the backpack.

Smiling evilly, Cleeve stood in front of Bobby and ran his huge hands over the boy's crimson pecs. Bobby looked angrily at Cleeve through blurred vision and a thin line of saliva dripped out of his mouth. Cleeve ran the tips of his big thumbs over the wounded tips of Bobby's nipples and breathed deeply. He looked into Bobby's tear filled eyes and for an iota of a second felt sorry for the kid…then they untied Bobby from the tree, leaving his upper body and arms roped tightly. The boy's shoulders were scraped and irritated from the tree bark. They turned Bobby around facing the tree, kicked his legs roughly apart, exposing his stretched rosebud of a hole and unzipped their hiking shorts. The bark from the tree was now irritating the fuck out of the boy's stomach area, his beaten up chest, and his aching cock and balls.

"Time for a good old fashioned fuck eh Cleeve?" Otis asked merrily as Cleeve stepped behind Bobby, his huge monster-sized cock hard, pulsing and in hand.

"Hell yeah," Cleeve grunted in a man's passion. "Whacking his tits and pecs and hearing this kid's screams really got me all worked up down here."

Cleeve unceremoniously pressed the tip of his huge cock against Bobby's hole and slid it home.

"AAAYYYRRRRR!!!" Bobby gasped loudly as Cleeve's cock speared him awfully.

"OH yeah, still all nice and moist back here boy," Cleeve quipped and slapped Bobby's butt cheeks real hard.

"BASTARDS, fucking lowlifes, fucking me all over again," Bobby snorted angrily.

Cleeve rammed the boy's hole super hard, pressing him meanly up against the tree, practically hoisting him off the ground with his huge manhood in Bobby's hole. Bobby felt beyond defiled, filled and impaled upon Cleeve's monster-sized sausage stick as it pulsed inside him.

"HOOORRRRRRR GOD!!!" Bobby roared, looking up at the sky, tears streaming out of his eyes.

As Cleeve fucked him Bobby pulled himself to his tiptoes, doing his best to endure every hard crashing thrust that the sadistic Cleeve jammed into him. Cleeve bounced Bobby against the tree, causing him to hit his forehead against it, making the kid's head spin as he fucked him and fucked him and then fucked him some more.

"AAAAYYYRRRRRRR PLEASE!!!" Bobby wailed at the heavens.

"Oh yeah, get ready you gorgeous fucking stud, because I'm about to let fly and fill this sexy shit chute of yours all over again," Cleeve panted and grabbed Bobby's hips real tight.

Thrusting feverishly now in and out of Bobby's hole Cleeve shot an ogre-sized load, and doing exactly what he had just said he would do, namely filling the boy's hole with it.

"OH yeah, yeah, real sexy manhole you got there boy, or in your case I guess we'll call it your boy-hole, ha!" Cleeve seethed madly, still thrusting in real hard and mercilessly. "Real hot and moist, like a velvet glove in there..."

When Cleeve was done his cock slipped out of Bobby's poor and broken aching hole. Before the boy could even think to lower himself from his tiptoes Otis' cock was inside him next.

"AAAAAHHHHHRRRRR NO, OH SHIT!!" Bobby screamed pitifully as he was slammed up against the tree again.

They each managed to fuck Bobby two times while he was pinned up against the tree. When they were done the boy was on his knees on the ground, his head hanging down, gasping, heaving and crying awfully, sweat drenching him. His muscular body was nearly a roadmap of scrapes and bruises and his hole was throbbing in a pain he had never known before as it embarrassingly dripped with the two men's cum. The clamps on his nipples tugged the nubs way down, really making his tender tits ache beyond reason. To Bobby it felt as if three pairs of tit clamps had been tightly fastened to his nipples.

"F-fuckers, fucking sadistic kidnappers," Bobby gasped, looking up at the two men through tear soaked eyes. "H-how the fuck can you do this to me???"

Smiling down at the boy, his cock still dangling semi hard out of his shorts, Cleeve wagged the monster sized phallus in Bobby's handsome face.

"C'mon boy, eat up," Cleeve said, slapping Bobby's face with his slimy cock.

Beaten and in total pain Bobby did not dare resist the man. At this point to resist would have meant something more severe than sucking a cock that had just been jammed up his ass. Bobby opened his mouth, stuck out his tongue, and slurped Cleeve's huge cock into his mouth.

"OH YEAH, suck that cock you handsome bastard," Cleeve grunted in total passion, doing a thrust-like dance as he now fucked the kid's face.

"Oh man Cleeve, making the boy suck your shit tasting cock, that is just plain awful," Otis chortled mockingly.

"Yeah, but look at the fucking kid, he's really into sucking my huge fucking meat," Cleeve gasped. "Whoever the fuck his master is must make him suck his shit tasting cock after he fucks him. The master must have trained him for it."

Cleeve placed a hand gently behind the boy's head and caressed it as Bobby went on sucking him like crazy. It was the gentlest gesture either of the men had bestowed on Bobby since getting the drop on him and snagging him from his job-site. Otis stepped behind Cleeve, rolled Cleeve's tee shirt up over his big nipples, and standing behind Cleeve reached around him and grabbed his over-sized nips.

"Oh yeah, that's it Otis, make my nips feel real good while the kid sucks me off," Cleeve panted, his head thrown back, his cock now down deep in Bobby's throat.

"Bet his nips aren't feeling all that good right about now," Otis said, gently fingering Cleeve's nipples. "What with the way we treated them and those clamps being on them for so long now."

The two men laughed hysterically and then Cleeve shot another big load, right down the boy's throat.

"OH YEAH, that's it you cock sucker, eat my damned ball juice," Cleeve grunted, his balls crashing against Bobby's chin as he came and came.

"RRRRMMMFFFFFFFF!!!" Bobby gasped and his head spun as his breath was momentarily cut off.

When he opened his eyes he saw that it was now Otis' cock in his mouth. He could not even recall Cleeve having taken his cock out of his mouth and Otis having shoved his in. Not even able to think about it Bobby simply knelt there as the two men took turns now fucking and fucking his mouth, making him swallow their slimy cum each time they came. By the time they were done the boy's mouth was a mess of cum and salty and musty tasting.

"OH man, can't fucking believe I came so many times," Cleeve panted, leaning up against the tree Bobby had been tethered to. "Damn Otis, his mouth is beautiful, and so fucking warm and soft, like I said, like velvet."

"Yeah, whoever this kid's master is really is one lucky son of a bitch," Otis said, giving each of Cleeve's nipples a kiss and rolling his tee shirt back down for him.

Bobby was still kneeling on the ground, his head hanging down as cum caked up all over his trembling lips. Small thin tears slid down his face and he whispered, "Master, I need you," low enough so that his two captors did not hear him. Bobby's plea sounded like a desperate silent prayer and he cried more as he saw Master Kent in his mind's eye. He knelt there, every part of him trembling with his lips now pursed as his delicate tears landed on the ground. Suddenly, he felt something pressing manly against his gaping and stretched very tortured hole. Jarred abruptly to his senses he reeled his head around and looked at the two men towering frighteningly over him from behind. When he realized that Cleeve was forcing the giant dildo from the night before into his hole he roared in tortured and awful agony.

"OHHHHRRRRRRR NO, no, not this again you bastards!! OH YOU FUCKING bastards!!!" Bobby screamed as Cleeve was actually lifting him up off the ground with the invasive device, using it as a handle of sorts that was jammed deep in the boy's poor hole. "OHHHHHRRRRR SSSSHHHHIIIITTTT…"

"Time to get back to our walk boy," Otis said as Cleeve lifted Bobby with the dildo, inch by torturous inch.

"OHHHHHRRR GAWD, GAWD," Bobby panted through clenched teeth as he was lifted to his feet.

"I told you this would come in handy Otis," Cleeve said and twisted the dildo around in Bobby's hole when the boy was finally on his fucked up and battered feet. "And you didn't want me to bring it along. Now, watch the boy dance."

Cleeve forced the dildo in further and Bobby's body arched forward and he doubled over in sheer agony. The two men laughed heartily as Bobby choked and nearly vomited. Cleeve pulled up on the dildo and Bobby was again standing up straight, tottering on his feet, his clamped nipples jiggling uncontrollably in pain and complete agony. His cock and balls swayed between his legs.

"Okay boy, let's start walking again," Cleeve commanded and Otis picked up the backpack and slung it over Bobby's back.

Holding the end of the dildo in hand Cleeve pushed Bobby along, further and deeper into the woods. Bobby's cock jutted out in front of him totally yet unbelievably rock hard from being relentlessly tortured and terrorized. He pissed as the dildo stretched his hole even further. He cried, was racked with sobs and made loud noises of pain as he plodded on…

While his boy was being horribly tortured Master Kent was at the police station talking with his cop buddy, Officer John McLaughlin. The cop told Kent that there was really not all that much that he or his buddies on the force could do for Bobby at the moment, explaining that they really didn't have proof that Cleeve and Otis had abducted his boy. Officer McLaughlin did tell Kent however that the job-site where Bobby had last been seen by two of his work buddies had been investigated by the police. What they had found was puddles of cum all over the floor. It looked as if a few guys had had a circle jerk of some kind there. Master Kent said that Bobby would never participate in something like that, going on to say softly to his buddy that the only time Bobby shoots his load is when he, as his master permits it. Officer McLaughlin looked at Kent across the desk and said what he suspected, that Bobby had been somehow forced to create that puddle of cum at the job-site. The cop went on to tell Kent that by the evening, if Bobby still hadn't shown up or at least called that he would file a missing person's report. He also added how that probably wouldn't be necessary because Cleeve and Otis never held onto a victim more than twenty four hours…according to what the police knew of the two men. Master Kent looked at his cop buddy snidely and said, "But you just said that you don't have proof that Cleeve and Otis have my boy." Officer McLaughlin looked at Master Kent helplessly…

While Officer McLaughlin was trying to put Master Kent's mind at ease poor Bobby was still being pushed along by Cleeve with that huge dildo wedged way up into his hole. Bobby's muscular and battered body was arched, his cock jutted out long and painfully fear hard in front of him and he was practically walking on his tiptoes. To make his situation even worse Otis was walking in front of the boy, holding the kid's cock ringed manhood in hand, stroking him as he plodded on.

"OHHHHRRRR fucking fucker, got my by my cock," Bobby gasped as Otis squeezed his cock hard, inflicting excruciating pain.

The boy knew that from the way Otis was handling him that if he shot a load how the pain would be overly excruciating. He also knew how much the huge dildo wedged in his hole and the clamps snapped on his nipples would drive him utterly batty after he shot a load, if he shot a load that is. But as they walked on and as Otis man handled his ringed cock Bobby felt it.

"OHHHRRRRRR GAWD, oh shit, oh fucking, fucking shit you guys," Bobby panted. "I-I'm goin' to cream right now you bastards!!" They stopped walking and Cleeve began meanly thrusting the dildo in and out of Bobby's hole as Otis squeezed and stroked the boy's poor aching cock.

"AAARRRHHHHHHHRRRRR!!!!" Bobby screamed as his juices spewed from his wounded cock, he screaming so loudly this time that a flock of birds flew out of a tree.

When he was done shooting his load Bobby hopped around in pain and misery as the dildo and the tit clamps practically drove him over the edge of sanity at that point.

"Man, can this boy dance," Cleeve said mockingly.

"AAAYYYYRRRRR!!!!" Bobby shrilled madly as he danced and tottered on his very much fucked up feet.

A short while later Cleeve yanked the dildo out of the boy's hole.

"TH-*thank you,*" Bobby whispered as the walls of his stretched hole seemed to twitch with a life of their own and he farted twice.

Without a word Cleeve took the backpack off Bobby's back and brought out a long length of rope. Bobby wondered what the fuck he was in for now...

The boy didn't have to wait long to find out because a few minutes later he found himself blindfolded and hanging upside down by his now securely tied ankles. Cleeve and Otis hoisted him up, up, and up on a tree branch and tied the slack of the rope off to another nearby tree.

"OHHHHHH SHIT, fuckers got me hanging like a damned slab of beef in a butcher's freezer," Bobby complained miserably, twisting on the end of the rope.

Then, Bobby was once more screaming royally in pain as the two men began paddling him with the round leather paddles. They rapped his poor welted and already red ass cheeks, the backs and fronts of his thighs, his crimson pecs, and his hugely muscular arms. Being blindfolded made it all the worse for the boy as he could not see where the next blow would be landing and was forced to concentrate on the horrid pain. Bobby's screams of torture and agony echoed through the woods as he hung there helplessly being beaten, being beaten for no apparent reason other than the fact that he was a beautiful stud of a boy who had unwittingly fallen victim to two madmen...

When Bobby thought for sure that he was about to pass out the two men stopped paddling him. He hung there gasping, heaving for breath, and crying big tears behind his blindfold.

"Man oh man Otis, when we give this boy back to his master he is going to be one very changed person," Cleeve said to his buddy, giving Bobby's reddened butt cheeks a squeeze.

The two men laughed mockingly and Bobby again whispered, "Master, I need you," softly enough so that the two men could not hear him. After cutting the boy down from the tree and taking the blindfold off him they sat him on a long fallen tree. Sitting on the ground in front of Bobby Cleeve opened another section of the backpack and brought out sandwiches and a couple of plastic bottles of mineral water.

"Lunch time boy," Cleeve said to Bobby.

Bobby simply looked at him blankly through blurred vision. They fed the boy two sandwiches, which he gobbled down vigorously. Then they made him drink a good amount of water. He gulped the water down vigorously as well.

"Feeling better boy?" Cleeve asked Bobby when they were all done eating. "I mean, this sure is one hell of a fucking workout we're putting you through here."

"This is no workout," Bobby spat at Cleeve, sounding totally indignant. "This is outright sadistic and unwarranted torture!! When the fucks are you two going to let me go man???"

Bobby looked down at his clamped nipples and his bruised and battered body. He choked back a loud sob.

"Fuckers," he whispered. "Look what you've done to me..."

The two men looked at each other and smiled.

"Bet you're thinking a lot about that master of yours eh boy?" Cleeve asked Bobby. "Probably you can't wait for us to hand you back over to him."

Bobby nodded and an awful feeling of helplessness suddenly consumed him.

"I wonder if he's thinking you've left him," Otis said snidely and meanly.

"He would not think that," Bobby replied angrily. "He knows how much I love him. He knows I would never leave him."

When they were done eating and drinking water they walked on a while more with Bobby between them (at that point every step the boy took was outright torture on his bruised and cut up feet) until they came to another very sizeable oak tree.

"Okay Otis, after this we'll start heading back," Cleeve said, looking menacingly at the boy.

Bobby wondered what was going to happen to him next...

In answer to his unvoiced question Bobby found himself hanging from a tree branch yet again, this time by his wrists. His muscular and well-toned body was stretched painfully taut his wrists pulled above him and tied off to the sturdy branch above him and his feet tightly tied at the ankles. His toes just about touched the ground as he hung there stretched out and in utter pain. When the two men had untied his upper body to get him into position he did not resist at all, all the fight had been beaten out of the poor boy. As he hung there Cleeve and Otis stood in front of him, licking, slurping, and sucking Bobby's rancid and stinking armpits.

"MMMMMM..." the two men crooned as they sucked the juice from the boy's bushy pits, giving the tips of his *still* clamped nipples a few hard squeezes as they did so.

Bobby gasped and screamed in tortured agony every time they squeezed his excessively sore nipples. He squirmed in horrid pain at the end of that rope as he hung like a side of beef in a butcher's freezer from that tree. The two men ran their hands all over him, squeezing the muscles in his stretched arms, reaching behind him and squeezing and jiggling his sweet butt cheeks, and tugging on his still cock ringed balls. Bobby's cock stuck out in front of him, long, wounded and somehow semi hard.

"Fuckers, eatin' my stinking pits as an after lunch treat eh?" Bobby asked the men sarcastically.

As they slurped the fuck out of his armpits Cleeve grabbed Bobby's aching cock and twisted it hard, twisted it till the boy screamed and the sound of his shrillness echoed through the woods...

When the two sadistic men had had enough of slurping and sucking the armpit juice out of the boy's pits his pit hairs were soaked with a mixture of his sweat and the two men's saliva. With evil looking smiles on their faces they each yanked a few of Bobby's armpit hairs out. Poor Bobby screeched and squealed in pain each time one of his pit hairs was yanked out.

"AAAAYYYYYRRRR SSSHIIITTT!!" Bobby roared as Cleeve pulled more than one hair at a time out of his pit. "FUCKERS just keep coming up with more and more ways to torture the fuck outa me!!!"

"Sure as shit boy, and when you see what we have in mind for you next you are not going to fucking believe it!" Cleeve said and snapped his fingers against Bobby's aching balls.

"OHHHRRRRRR..." Bobby whimpered loudly as Otis yanked out a few more of his armpit hairs and Cleeve jiggled his balls with the tips of his fingers.

"Okay Otis, enough with those stinking armpit hairs of his," Cleeve said authoritatively. "Tie a blindfold on the kid and then we'll really get him howling."

"What do you have in mind for the boy now?" Otis asked Cleeve with a grin as he took a long white cloth from his pocket.

"Nothing he's going to like, that is for fucking sure," Cleeve said fiendishly.

Bobby shivered in fear anew as Otis leered at him menacingly and tied the blindfold over his eyes, plunging the kid into darkness. It should be mentioned at this point that when Master Kent's boy, Bobby rides the train to work everyday he keeps an isoflex squeeze ball in his backpack. While riding to work on the train he squeezes the ball, alternating it between his hands. Being that Bobby works with his hands all day this keeps them good and strong and it is also a definite stress reliever. Before abducting Bobby Cleeve had helped himself to the isoflex ball from the boy's backpack along with the tit clamps he had had in there. Cleeve took the ball now from his backpack and he and Otis squatted down on their haunches a few feet away from where Bobby was dangling in agony from the tree branch.

"Okay, you're really going to get a charge out of this," Cleeve said to Otis. "And so will he."

For a few seconds Bobby hung there in silent darkness, but then, Cleeve threw the isoflex ball at him, aiming for his balls.

"AAAYYYRRRRRRRRRRRR!!!!" Bobby yowled like a trapped animal when his isoflex ball smacked hard against his poor aching balls.

Bobby involuntarily took a hop backwards on his toes.

"Get back into position boy!!" Cleeve ranted at Bobby.

As stinging pain shot through Bobby's balls he moved himself slowly forward on his bound feet, using only his toes as they barely made contact with the ground.

"Okay Otis, your turn," Bobby heard Cleeve say.

Bobby heard Otis run over to him to retrieve the isoflex ball, then dash back over to Cleeve.

"Okay, aim for his nuts, good and fucking hard," Cleeve instructed Otis.

"OOOHHHHHHHHH no, *no, not again!!*" Bobby gasped and then he felt the stinging pain seer through his balls and up into his stomach area a second time when Otis flung the isoflex ball at him.

"AAAAYYYYYRRRR!!!!" Bobby squealed again in the awful misery.

He leaned his head back through his stretched arms and his blindfolded eyes stared up at heaven.

"*Oh God, oh good God,*" Bobby whispered, heaving, his teeth clenched and tears soaking his blindfold.

The two men flung the isoflex ball two more times each at Bobby's balls and he nearly passed out from the unthinkable pain of it. Actually, the poor boy thought for sure that they were going to kill him at that point, him thinking that he would never see Master Kent again. That thought caused Bobby more pain than any isoflex ball being thrown at his balls ever could.

"Okay Otis, that's enough," Cleeve said, suddenly sounding worried. "His balls won't be able to stand another blow from that thing."

Bobby heaved again for breath and screamed and cried loudly, sounding insane by then, the sounds emanating from him echoing in the woods...

A short while later the two men cut the boy down from the tree. He knelt in front of Cleeve and Otis with his hands roped behind him and the blindfold off him as they towered over him. Bobby was trembling like a leaf and crying profusely, his head hanging down over his captor's muddied hiking boots.

"Okay boy, we'll start heading back now," Cleeve said. "Fuck knows you've really been through *it.*"

Bobby nodded in agreement, not looking up at the two men. To his utter disbelief he leaned down and kissed each of Cleeve and Otis' boots.

"Don't be so fucking glad to be heading back yet boy," Cleeve said meanly, the sounds of concern suddenly gone from his tone. "There's still the walk back for you to endure. And believe you me *that* is going to be just as hard as the walk coming here."

Bobby sniveled, his tears landing on one of Cleeve's boots. He quickly lapped it off for fear of punishment.

"Shit Cleeve, you mean we're going to torture this kid going back too?" Otis asked merrily.

"Sure as shit Otis, sure as fucking shit," Cleeve said, reached down, and hauled Bobby roughly to his battered feet.

"Man, but we sure as fuck are working hard today," Otis said mockingly.

Bobby stood there before the two men, a sweaty, stinking and beaten mess. Cleeve slicked the boy's mussed and sweat soaked hair back as Otis looked at his semi hard cock, a wicked grin on his face. Otis plucked a long, thin stemmed dandelion from a nearby bush, grabbed Bobby's balls real tight which caused the boy's cock to go fear stiff, and jammed the stem of the flower into Bobby's cock slit.

"AAAYYYRRRRR!!!" Bobby wailed and hopped around in agony, the flower sticking out of his cock hole.

"There you go boy, don't ever say we never gave you flowers," Otis said tauntingly.

Bobby clenched his teeth, squeezed his eyes shut in pain, and screamed shrilly, "You sick fucks!!"

Leading the way Cleeve began the walk back followed by Bobby with Otis behind him. Beads of piss formed around the flower stem in Bobby's cock hole and dripped to the ground as he trudged on. Otis didn't take that flower out of the boy's cock hole till they were half-way to the house. And before taking it out he held Bobby's poor aching balls with one hand and with his other hand he jammed the flower stem in and out of the boy's cock hole, literally fucking Bobby's piss hole with the flower stem. When he finally did yank it out the two men stood there laughing hysterically as big thick beads of hot yellow piss erupted almost involuntarily from the boy's slit, landing on his upper body as his cock was pointing straight up. Bobby danced in pain as he pissed as the inside of his cock felt like it was on fire.

"Ha, look at that shit Cleeve," Otis chortled. "Got the kid pissin' hot and hard."

"AAAYYYRRRRR!!!" Bobby screamed.

While Bobby was dancing in pain and pissing all over himself Master Kent was headed home from police headquarters. His cop buddy had somehow managed to reassure the leather master that his boy would be returned to him, if it were Cleeve and Otis that had him. Officer McLaughlin had gone into vivid detail about the other men who had reported being abducted by Cleeve and Otis and how they had all been released before they had been missing for even twenty-four hours. Their pattern never seemed to change. Although, to keep Master Kent as calm as possible Officer McLaughlin did not tell the leather master about the young upstate trooper who had gone missing more than a month ago at that point. Master Kent's cop buddy was sure it was Cleeve and Otis who had nabbed Officer Scott Reed (**from the story "Captured Cop"**) but why they had not yet released him was still a mystery. When Master Kent asked his cop buddy what sort of condition the abducted men had been in when they were released he simply looked at Kent helplessly from behind his desk. With that thought in mind Master Kent walked despondently into his and Bobby's house. To Master Kent the place itself seemed to be missing Bobby just as much as he was. Without Bobby there the house actually seemed totally empty. Kent looked over at the framed photograph of his boy on the coffee table and his breath caught in his throat. Just the thought of his special boy drove Master Kent wild...

Bobby, at that moment was having more than his share of difficulty walking due to the large, fallen, and monstrously heavy tree branch that Cleeve and Otis had slung across the boy's broad shoulders. His wrists were tied off to the ends of it as he plodded along slowly, lugging the tree branch. The backpack that Bobby had been carrying earlier was dangling off the end of the branch strewn across his shoulders.

"Jeez Cleeve, that was a stroke of genius on your part, to have the kid move that fallen tree branch from where it was," Otis said.

"Sure thing Otis, we wouldn't want any campers or hikers accidentally tripping over it," Cleeve chuckled and looked at Bobby. "Think of this as doing your good deed for the day boy..."

Every time the weight of the large tree branch bore down and slowed Bobby up the two men got him moving by rapping his ass cheeks hard with their leather paddles. As Bobby walked with his head hung down mosquitoes and flies landed all over him again and feasted heartily...

Finally, after what seemed like hours they arrived back at Cleeve's huge house. The two men untied the tree branch from Bobby's shoulders, tossed it to the ground, and quickly roped his arms back up behind him. His shoulders were now also a mess of bruises and deep scrape from having carried that tree branch through the woods. It was nearing evening and the sun was beginning to set. At the sight of Cleeve and Otis' van the boy's eyes filled with tears of joy.

"Oh God," he whispered.

"So boy," Cleeve said, placing a hand one of Bobby's shoulders. "Where do you and this master of yours live?"

Bobby looked at Cleeve through tear soaked eyes of anger and pain...

That night, in their house, Master Kent was sitting in the living room with his cop buddy, Officer John McLaughlin. The cop had stopped by on his way home from headquarters to check on the distraught leather master, and of course to see if Kent's boy had somehow contacted him. Officer McLaughlin had just worked a double shift and he was mentally and physically exhausted. But he could not see himself going home until his friend's boy was safe. He sat across from Master Kent in a living room chair dressed sharply and regally in his navy blue uniform, his tie fastened to his shirt and his black patent leather shoes all shiny looking. He sat holding the eight by ten framed picture of Bobby that had been taken recently.

"He really is a great looking kid Kent," the cop said. "I sure hope I'm wrong and that those two bastards, Cleeve and Otis didn't get their hands on him."

"Then what other explanation is there?" Master Kent asked in response. "Bobby wouldn't just up and disappear without some sort of an explanation."

"Sorry, but I can't think of one," the cop said and placed the picture frame back on the coffee table in front of him.

"Seeing as you're off duty I'll get you a beer," Kent said, getting to his feet. "It's the least I can so since you've been working on this for me."

"Yeah, that sounds good, thanks," the cop said.

As Master Kent was walking to the kitchen he heard a low moan coming from outside the door to the house. He stopped walking, stepped closer to the door, listened, and heard it again. It was the sound of someone in total anguish. The leather master looked apprehensively across the room at his cop buddy and dashed to the door, the cop hot on his heels, his hand over the gun in his holster. Master Kent opened the door and there was Bobby, naked, kneeling on the floor, his arms roped tightly and painfully up behind him. His upper body was roped tight as well, his feet bound and a sock was crammed in his mouth with a rope tied over it, thoroughly gagging him. His nipples were still clamped, his cock and balls were still ringed and to Master Kent's horror as he looked at the boy in front of the door he was a mess of purple bruises, scrapes and mean looking scratches.

"Holy fuck, Bobby!!" Master Kent roared and he and his cop buddy gently and carefully lifted the boy to his bound feet.

"MMMFFFFFFFF!!!" Bobby panted miserably behind his gag and arched his body forward.

Looking behind him Master Kent saw the reason why Bobby had just arched his body in such a manner. There was a huge over-sized dildo wedged deep in the boy's hole with a piece of paper clipped to the end of it.

"Goddamned bastards," Master Kent ranted when he saw the size of the invasive atrocity tormenting his boy's hole.

Kent slowly pulled the dildo out of the Bobby's hole, the poor boy mewling and screaming behind his gag.

"Let's get him inside and untied, fast!" Master Kent ranted, slamming and locking the door.

"Shit, it looks like they really had a time working him over," Officer McLaughlin said as he and Kent lifted Bobby and carried him over to the couch.

They laid the boy gently on the couch and quickly began unty-ing him. When Kent got the sock/gag out of his mouth Bobby whim-pered in awful pain but his eyes told Master Kent how happy he was to see him and to be back with him as well. Master Kent took the tit clamps off his boy's nipples and the poor kid screamed in pain as the blood rushed back into his wounded nubs. The cop did the honors of removing Bobby's cock ring from his cock and balls. When the boy was completely untied he sat up, threw himself into Master Kent's arms and held onto him tighter than ever before in all their time together. Bobby smelled something awful but to Master Kent that didn't matter. At the moment the boy needed him and he would not let go of him.

"I-I'm sorry Master," Bobby squeaked in his mentor's ear. "Th-th-they…"

"It's okay Bobby, you have nothing to be sorry about," Master Kent whispered in the boy's ear, choking on his own tears and gently kissed the boy's cheek "You're home now boy, you're home."

"Bobby, was it Cleeve and Otis?" Officer McLaughlin asked the boy.

Bobby nodded and at the mention of the names Cleeve and Otis Bobby clung tighter still to Master Kent, the boy looking despon-dently at the huge dildo on the coffee table, where his master had dropped it after extracting it from his hole. Officer McLaughlin donned latex gloves, took the note off it and read it.

"What does it say?" Master Kent asked him. "Read it to me."

"Dear Master Kent," the cop began reading. "Thank you for the use of your boy. He is real sweet. We mean that from a literal sense, real sweet, and he sure as fuck can take it. You've trained him well. Let us know if he wants to see us again in the future and we will be happy to put the screws to him a second and even a third time for you."

As Officer McLaughlin read the letter Bobby clung tighter to Master Kent, as if his very life depended upon it.

"For now we are returning him to you," the cop went on reading. "He is a little bruised and worked over, but in a day or so he will be as good as new, if not better. Signed C&O."

Officer McLaughlin put the note down on the coffee table and looked at Bobby.

"They brought you here?" Master Kent's buddy asked in shock.

Bobby nodded.

"Maybe they haven't gotten too far," the cop said, peeled the latex gloves off his hands and dropped them on the coffee table next to the letter he'd just read and headed for the door. "Maybe with some luck I can still catch them. Bobby, was it a big black van that they had?"

"Y-yeah," Bobby replied. "I-I'm sorry, I-I didn't think to try to get the license plate number."

"It's okay kid, you did good remembering the color," Kent's cop buddy said and then looked at the leather master. "Kent, get him to a hospital. I'm going to see about trying to nail those two fuckers!! Don't touch the note they left with Bobby. I want it for evidence."

He dashed out of the apartment, slamming the door loudly behind him.

"N-no hospital Master Kent," Bobby whispered. "Please Sir, I'll be okay, just hold me Master Kent, *I need you…I need you…"*

Master Kent stifled his tears, kissed the top of Bobby's head and held him tight and close as the boy sobbed and shook uncontrollably. Seeing his boy in that state was the first time Master Kent swore revenge on the two men known as Cleeve and Otis, the two men who had done this awful thing to his special, special boy…

While Bobby and Master Kent sat on the couch, reunited, Officer John McLaughlin was driving his police cruiser through the dark streets, desperately trying to find the van that matched the description of Cleeve and Otis'. Officer John McLaughlin, six foot two, thirty years old, heavily muscled, with dark military style cut hair and dark eyes, an ex-marine, drove slowly and methodically through the streets. His huge ham-like hands gripped the steering wheel angrily.

"Shit, not a sign of the van anywhere," the cop said in frustration. "More than likely they're gone already. Probably dropped that poor kid off and took off back to where they come from like bats out of hell."

He pounded a big fist on the steering wheel and not wanting to give up so quickly drove down toward the waterfront, a local and sleazy hangout for people like Cleeve and Otis. As the anger coursed through him his bowling ball sized-biceps and massive chest muscles bulged, straining against his tight fitting, navy blue police uniform shirt and tie. The cop stopped the car and saw not a black van as Bobby had said, but rather a dark blue one parked in a no-parking area.

"Okay, looks like I'm going to wind up the night giving this joker a ticket for illegal parking," the frustrated cop seethed and stepped out of his cruiser.

He walked slowly over to the passenger side of the van and looked in the window. He saw no one in the vehicle. As he was about to step to the front of the van to check the plate number he was suddenly clacked hard on the head from behind with a lead pipe. His police cap somewhat cushioned the blow, but he was still knocked to the ground, horribly stunned and his head spinning.

"You see Otis, I told you that if we hung out here long enough some great looking hunk of cop meat would wander around for us to nab," Cleeve said to his buddy as they stood over their newest conquest.

"O-Otis?" Officer McLaughlin gasped as his hands were locked behind him with his own handcuffs.

Cleeve yanked the fallen cop to his knees by the back of his uniform shirt collar.

"AAACCHHHHH!!!" Officer McLaughlin croaked as his shirt choked him.

Cleeve raised the pipe and again clacked the poor cop over the head, this time sending him to dreamland.

"Let's get started Otis," Cleeve said. "This cop has a long night ahead of him.

Part Two
The Use and Abuse of Officer McLaughlin
(1987)

It was now ten AM. Master Kent was in the kitchen brewing a pot of coffee after having set out bagels and bialys on the table. He was dressed in a pair of old denim shorts, a black tank top, sweat socks and sneakers. As he stood facing the coffee maker he heard Bobby come slowly and softly into the kitchen. The leather man turned and saw his boy. He was standing in the archway of the kitchen, leaning against the sidewall, dressed only in a fresh pair of white Calvin Klein boxer shorts. He was all cleaned up from the night before, having taken a very lengthy hot shower. Every time Bobby screamed in pain from the soap getting in his bloody wounds Master Kent's heart broke. At the sight of his boy standing there Master Kent's breath caught in his throat. Actually, every time the rugged leather man looked at his beyond handsome boy his breath caught in his throat. In Kent's opinion Bobby was handsome enough to make grown men cry. He could not imagine why anyone would want to hurt him in the way's that Cleeve and Otis had. It was outside his comprehension. The two men looked at each other for the briefest of moments before Master Kent turned away from the coffee maker.

"How are you doing?" Kent asked as he slowly walked over to Bobby. "Did you sleep okay?"

Bobby simply nodded, looking blankly at his master. Kent had lain awake most of the night before, watching the boy sleep. It reminded him a bit of when they had first met and he would watch the boy sleep. In Master Kent's opinion Bobby looks like an angel when he sleeps. The boy's body was very bruised and scraped up from what he had endured the day before. His shoulders were thoroughly scratched up from the tree bark he had been tied against and from the heavy tree branch he had been made to carry. His stomach and chest regions were also very battered looking. His nipples were still very swollen from the clamps that Cleeve and Otis had left on them practically all day. Master Kent fumed at that, seeing as it's always fun to clamp a guy's nipples while working him over sexually. The sensations are a mixture of erotic pain and ecstasy. But after a guy has shot his load you have to get said clamps off his nipples, fast. Master Kent taught Bobby that leaving tit clamps on a guy's nipples after he's cum could really drive the poor fucker crazy.

"You being the poor fucker at this moment," Master Kent had said to Bobby, smiling lovingly down at him as he lay strapped to a table after he had taken the tit clamps off Bobby's nipples after the boy had shot his pent-up load.

Bobby told his master how Cleeve and Otis had jacked him off numerous times and had left his poor nipples tightly clamped. Master Kent could not believe that the poor kid didn't lose his mind. In his manner of training Bobby when he used tit clamps on the boy during a scene he always took them off him the second after he shot his load. Master Kent always said he believed in strong training for his boy, but he also believed in not causing him undue pain and anguish. Besides handsome Kent's boy is strong, extremely strong willed as well. His cock looked pretty sore and his balls were not as swollen as they had looked the night before. His feet were still very much scraped up though, but the bleeding had stopped at least, much to Master Kent's relief. The poor kid couldn't even put on a pair of socks his feet were so battered. His butt cheeks (which Master Kent could not see from where he was standing at the moment) were still pretty sore as well and his hole, well, that, in Master Kent's opinion was a whole other story. By going there Cleeve and Otis, in the leather man's beliefs had signed their death warrants. He knew that it would take more than a few days for Bobby's hole to feel better. Walking slowly toward the boy Kent held his big muscular arms out, open and invitingly to him. Bobby took a few steps forward and threw himself into his master's arms. The kid was shaking again. Master Kent held him tightly and kissed and kissed the top of his head. His beautiful silky hair smelled of shampoo and was still slightly damp under Kent's lips.

"I love you Master Kent," Bobby whispered, hugging his master tight. "I-I'm so s-sorry."

"Bobby, shh, you have nothing to be sorry about," Kent replied. "I told you that last night. It wasn't your fault boy."

As Master Kent held him the boy let his tears flow. They landed on Kent's shirt, wetting the front of it. The burly leather man was fighting to choke back his own tears. It was rare that he would cry. Master

Kent is the kind of hard-core guy who does not usually like to show his emotions all that openly. But seeing his boy in the physical and mental pain that he was currently in totally broke the rugged guy's heart. Looking straight ahead at the framed picture of Bobby on the coffee table, the way he was smiling so beautifully in that picture made it hard for Kent to hold back his tears.

"Good God almighty Bobby," Master Kent said in a husky tone of voice. "I love you so much, so damned much that I cannot even describe it to you boy."

Bobby held tighter to his master as he spoke, the palms of his hands pressed against Kent's back.

"I'll kill those two fuckers for what they did to you," Kent said and again kissed Bobby on the top of his head. "I swear I will." Bobby pulled away slightly and looked up into his master's tear and rage filled eyes. He nodded his head "no" from side to side and said, "You can't Master Kent. Th-they'll never be caught, *never*. I can't explain what I mean by that, but I know I'm right. There's something evilly supernatural about Cleeve and Otis."

"We'll see Bobby, we'll see," Master Kent said, rubbing the tip of his thumb through the boy's tears. "I'm just glad you're home and safe."

"Me too Master Kent," Bobby whispered and slammed himself against his master, hugging him tightly again.

Kent hugged Bobby and held onto him so tightly that he was afraid that the boy would not be able to breathe. When he tried to loosen his hold just a bit on Bobby the boy clung to him tighter. He kissed his master's chest a couple of times as he held onto him.

"You hungry?" Kent asked Bobby, his hand placed gently on the back of his head.

The boy nodded that he was.

"Do you think you can eat something?" Master Kent asked.

Again the boy nodded...

A few moments later the two men were sitting at the table, cups of steaming coffee and plates with bagels and cream cheese in front of them. Bobby's hands had stopped trembling somewhat after a few bights.

"My buddy John went after Cleeve and Otis last night," Master Kent said as Bobby swallowed a bight of bagel.

"Sir, he, he's the cop that was here last night when Cleeve and

Otis dropped me at the door?" Bobby asked, sounding disturbed.

"Yeah, why, what's the problem?" Kent asked the boy.

"Have you heard from him since last night?" Bobby asked, sounding nervous.

"Well no, to tell you the truth I hadn't thought about him much, seeing as you needed me more than anything at the moment," Master Kent said. "Selfish of me maybe but..."

"Master Kent, *they got him,* I'm sure of it," Bobby said sounding angry and terrified at the same time, putting his bagel down on his plate. "Oh God Master Kent, those two bastards nabbed your good buddy Officer McLaughlin!"

"Bobby," Master Kent said, reaching and grabbing the boy's again trembling hand. "You don't know that. And besides, John is very resourceful."

"Master Kent so am I," Bobby said, looking at his master intensely. "But resourceful as I am, look what the fuck happened to me. Oh shit, poor Officer McLaughlin."

"Bobby, I'll call the precinct," Kent offered. "I am sure that by now John has Cleeve and Otis in custody.

Bobby simply nodded "no." Kent let go of the boy's hand, stood up, and walked over to the phone on the wall. Kent dialed his buddies' desk number. It rang two times before a male voice responded.

"Officer McLaughlin's desk, this is Officer Robinson speaking, may I help you?" the cop asked.

"This is Kent, how are you Robinson?" Master Kent said in friendly reply.

"Just fine Kent, and you?" the cop asked in return.

"Not so bad," the leather man quickly said. "Listen, is John there? I need to ask him something."

"Funniest thing Kent, he's not here and he hasn't called in sick or late or anything," Officer Robinson said. "I know he pulled a late night last night, but whenever he's going to be late or out he always calls."

"Shit..." Master Kent whispered.

"Is something wrong Kent?" Robinson asked, suddenly sounding very alert. "Is there something I should know? If one of our cop brothers is in trouble I need to know, *right now."*

Before replying Kent sat back down and pulled his chair close to Bobby's. He gently stroked the back of the boy's neck.

"Robinson, listen to me carefully," Master Kent said and began telling the cop about Bobby's abduction, his torture, his release, and how Officer McLaughlin had then gone in pursuit of Cleeve and Otis.

As Kent spoke Bobby leaned in close and the leather man held his boy tight...

While Kent was speaking to Officer Robinson, Officer John McLaughlin was at that moment trapped at the sleazy waterfront area. Still locked in his own handcuffs he had been stripped of his uniform pants, his underpants and his black patent leather shoes. The cop was sitting on the ground tied up to a utility post facing his two captors. The hunky officer was wearing just his knee length navy blue socks and the upper portion of his uniform, his shirt undone and his clip-on tie dangling off the side of it.

"Ohhhhhh man, m-my poor fucking head," John whimpered.

"Looks like he's comin' around Cleeve," John heard Otis saying as if from very far away.

Cleeve laughed meanly at the sight of the huge cop tied up and helpless at their feet. The sense of power over the captured officer of the law was more powerful than the sense the two men had gotten when they had captured Bobby the day before. Both Cleeve and Otis' cocks were stiff and dangling semi hard out of their jeans along with their big juicy cum chocked balls. Cleeve had a fiendish look on his face as the cop slowly came to and he thought of all the humiliating things that he and Otis and perhaps some others as well down there at the waterfront would put the handsome officer through.

"F-feels like I was hit by a goddamned truck," Officer McLaughlin gurgled as his head spun. "H-hey, what the fucking fuck is going on here? My hands are fucking cuffed behind me and I'm all tied up!! FUCKING FUCK!!"

As Officer John McLaughlin took in the fact that he was indeed all tied and handcuffed he was further shocked to realize that the lower portion of his uniform had been stripped off him. His pants and underpants had been tossed atop a nearby garbage pail along with his gun belt, baton and radio, which had been turned off at that point. No way of contacting headquarters he quickly surmised miserably. His police cruiser was nowhere in sight. Obviously after having captured him, Cleeve and Otis had quickly spirited the cop away to a more secluded spot in the waterfront area where they could get their jollies with him.

"*Fuck, what the hell is going on?*" John blurted and at the sound of the two men standing over him chuckling meanly he slowly looked upwards. "Shit, you two, you've got to be Cleeve and his mindless buddy Otis."

"Good to meet you too Officer Stupid McLaughlin," Otis responded. "Mindless am I? Who's the cop locked in his own god-damned handcuffs?"

The cop saw how they were looking down at his well muscled body and his cock and balls of huge size that they seemed like they should have belonged to a small pony rather than the handsome trapped officer.

"Man, he really is hung like a horse Cleeve," Otis commented. Terror mixed with rage filled the cop's piercing dark eyes as he took in the sight of Cleeve and Otis' stiffening cocks dangling out of their jeans.

"Sure as shit Otis," Cleeve laughed. "But for tonight he's a pussy..."

"That poor kid you kidnapped wasn't enough for you yesterday huh?" John seethed through clenched teeth. "You had to pick on a cop next!!"

"Officer McLaughlin, you are not the first cop we've gotten our hands on, nor will you be the last," Cleeve said.

John nodded his head from side to side, looking away from his captors and grinning stupidly he said, "H-holy fucking shit, *what a miserable twist of fate this is!*"

"And just what the fuck is that supposed to mean hot cop?" Cleeve asked, nudging the trapped cop's cock and balls with the tip of his work boot, beads of piss dripping from his hard cock and landing on the officer's leg.

"I, you bastards," John said as he sat there tied to the post before the two men, his long muscular legs spread out in front of him. "You two depraved maniacs kidnapped that kid, Bobby is his name, and you really fucked him over! God, that poor guy! I'm the cop who came after you after you dropped Bobby off at his leather master's house!"

Cleeve and Otis looked at each other in disbelief.

"H-holy fuck Cleeve!" Otis blurted in stupid sounding astonishment. "Now what were the chances of us nabbing the cop that had come after *us*? What a fucked up joke on him!"

"Sure looks that way," Cleeve said as he looked down at the captured cop and rubbing his own chin, seeming to mull it over. "As that old song says the hunter gets captured by the game."

"What are we going to do Cleeve?" Otis asked.

"We are going to do exactly what we planned on doing Otis my man," Cleeve said meanly. "We are going to have some real mean fun with a tough New York City cop. Fuck man, just look at this fucking stud, total macho man and total shit head all rolled up in a nice big cocked, big balled, big muscular package. That sweet master's boy that we got our hands on was a nice appetizer. He also doesn't know where the fuck my house is! We brought him there blindfolded and in a crate remember? And this cop ain't comin' to my house, no fucking way. What we're gonna do to him gets done right here at the waterfront area!"

"You fucking lowlife bastards, you tortured that poor kid beyond reason!!" John roared angrily.

"And we're going to do the same fucking thing to you Officer Stupid!!" Cleeve yelled and reached down to rap John hard across his ruggedly handsome face, knocking him into another stupor.

"OOOFFFFFFF!!" the cop gasped as the back of his head hit the post, this time his hat not on his head to cushion the blow. "UHHHNNNNN...wh-when I'm out of this you two are going to jail for a long fucking time!!"

Cleeve reached down again, grabbed the cop by his askew tie and shirt collar and again rapped the back of his head against the post.

"UUUCCCHHHHH," John grunted miserably.

"You'll have to get out of it first cop," Cleeve seethed as he held the cop's throat tight, squeezing it.

"AAAAACCCHHHHH..." the trapped cop croaked as his head spun.

"And may I also say that that master's boy that we nabbed was a *real delectable piece of ass!* Lucky fucking guy whoever his master is. That kid really adores his master!"

"Y-you sadistic fucks," John whimpered as his head again spun and Cleeve let go of his throat. That kid, uhhhhhhhhh, that kid is one of the gentlest and kindest people I have ever known! If you knew what he's been through in his life, God!!! OHHHHH, wh-what you two did to him is unforgivable!"

"We're not looking for forgiveness cop," Cleeve said snidely.

"Fuck you man, you two are under arrest right this minute!!"

John bellowed.

"You know cop, being that you're stripped the way we got you, you just don't come across all that convincingly," Cleeve laughed, reached down and again rapped the captured cop hard across the face.

This time as the cop screamed out in pain, his mouth open wide as he yelled out, Cleeve quickly squatted down and fed the officer his dangling hard cock. Cleeve's huge manhood slid halfway into the startled cop's craw.

"RRRRRMMMFFF..." Officer McLaughlin sputtered around the huge invasion as it filled his mouth and forced his jaws wide.

Cleeve grabbed the cop's head and forced his cock deeper into John's mouth. The cop gasped crazily at having his mouth raped with what felt like it had to be at least ten inches of man-meat but once Cleeve's cock slid in even more the officer found himself going to work. Humiliating as it was his lips and tongue started working Cleeve's cock for all they were worth. The cop felt as if his mouth was impaled on the gargantuan manhood as Cleeve fed it to him inch by giant inch. Otis' eyes were open wide in anticipation as he watched his good buddy having his cock sucked. He stroked his own manhood, getting it ready for its turn at bat in the cop's craw. Officer McLaughlin's lips pushed inwards with each of Cleeve's thrusts and they pulled back each time Cleeve would slightly withdraw his spearing cock.

"HHRRRRMMFFFF..." the cop choked and grunted angrily as he ate Cleeve's cock.

"Oh yeah Cleeve, he may not admit it but he loves sucking cock this cop we snagged," Otis laughed.

"Yeah, he's doing great, obviously this ain't his first time chowin' on some big beef stick," Cleeve drawled in man's passion. "Fuck, all the times we shot our loads with that master's boy was just a warm-up for what we'll feed this cop both front and rear."

"YYUUUUMMFFFF..." the cop prattled as he deep throated Cleeve's cock, looking upwards at Cleeve's mocking face and the star filled sky.

"That's it Officer Stupid, eat my cock and I'll feed you some sticky juice," Cleeve demanded as he held the cop's ears and fucked and fucked his mouth.

Officer McLaughlin felt his cheeks puff out still more and they glowed with total shame over this entire twisted turn of events. But as Cleeve did his dirty work the captured cop was even more humiliated to realize that his own cock was starting to stand up at full mast. Officer John McLaughlin secretly realized that his most erotic fantasy of being a "captured cop" was being woefully realized right there down by the sleazy waterfront. As the scent of seawater filled the air the taste of Cleeve's man juices suddenly filled the cop's mouth. Suddenly, with the sound of a lion in passion Cleeve shot his giant load into the cop's suckling mouth. He thrust his hips forward till his manhood was jammed down the cop's throat. The cop reluctantly swallowed every drop of Cleeve's gift to him, his Adam's apple bobbing up and down as he did so.

"AAAAAARRRRHHH, yeah, fucking A, fucking hot cop we got here, eat my load you stud..." Cleeve swore as he fed Officer McLaughlin what felt to the cop was an endless mess of thick goop.

"GGGRRRRRMMMMMFFFF..." was the sound that emanated from the cop as he felt Otis' hand on his cock.

"Hey Cleeve, the cop must really like what you're doin' to him, look at this, he's about to cum," Otis laughed as he stroked a load out of Officer McLaughlin's erection.

The cop felt his own load slopping from his cock and landing on the ground in front of him as Cleeve slowly withdrew his temporarily spent cock from his mouth. A few moments later with the taste of Cleeve's jazz filling his mouth and throat, with the remnants of it dripping from his trembling lips and breathing heavily the cop sat there while Cleeve and Otis stood over him looking totally triumphant.

"What's the matter cop?" Otis asked as he looked at John's softening meat stick as it dribbled out the last beads of his juices. "You don't like the taste of ball juice? Could have fooled me the way you shot that load just now..."

"You fuckers, you fucking bastards," the cop ranted and as he spoke Cleeve's cum dripped from his lips onto his rumpled uniform shirt as his huge chest heaved up and down. "I will see to it that you do not get away with this..."

"We'll see about that cop," Cleeve laughed. "Meanwhile, you got more cock to suck. Otis my man?"

As Otis stepped up to the plate with his huge cock in hand aimed at John's gaping mouth Master Kent and Bobby had finished breakfast. Kent was just hanging up the phone a second time with Officer Robinson, after the cop had called the leather man back. Bobby was seated on the couch as Kent came into the living room.

"That was Officer Robinson on the phone," he said, not sounding happy at all.

"Sir, what did he say?" Bobby asked.

"They found John's cruiser," Master Kent replied. "It had been abandoned a few blocks from the waterfront but he was nowhere to be found."

Bobby, sitting there now dressed in denim shorts, white sweat socks (which he had slid slowly and agonizingly onto his poor battered feet) and a white tee shirt looked at his master with fear in his eyes, fear for their good friend Officer John McLaughlin, knowing firsthand the tortures he faced at the hands of the maniacal Cleeve and Otis.

"The cruiser had been vandalized," Master Kent on. "But as I said, no sign of John anywhere."

"Master Kent, Sir, did Robinson say that they thought Cleeve and Otis got him?" Bobby asked as Kent sat down next to him.

"Yeah, he said that," Kent replied. "Shit, this is all too much to be believed.

"He didn't call in to the station that he was in pursuit of two very dangerous men when he went after them?" Bobby asked, seeming to be staring straight ahead into space.

"I guess not," Kent said. "I suppose you can say that John ran off half-cocked, hell bent on catching them, and he didn't think to call it in."

Master Kent and Bobby looked at each other then and the leather man gathered his boy into his arms, holding him tight. Bobby wrapped his arms around his master and hugged him fiercely.

"Just the thought of those two animals' hands on you makes me want to kill them Bobby," the leather master whispered in his boy's ear.

Bobby looked at Kent and pressed his lips against his loving master's. The two men kissed long and hard, hugging each other tighter and tighter.

"We may have to go down to headquarters boy," Kent said, stroking Bobby's beautiful silky hair. "Robinson may want to ask you some questions.

Bobby nodded that he would go and kissed Kent again on the lips.

"I called my boss when I woke up earlier," Bobby said as Kent held him close, hugging him. "I told him I would be taking a few days off for personal reasons. I have the time coming to me so it really wasn't a problem at all."

The boy then pressed his exquisite lips, his lips that Master Kent treasured each time they kissed, against his master's lips and the two men kissed again, long and hard, their tongues exploring each other's mouths. They sat there on the couch like that holding and kissing each other for what seemed like quite a long while. The boy didn't seem to want to let go of his master and Kent had no problem with fulfilling the boy's wish. Bobby pressed his hands against the back of Kent's huge neck and kissed his master harder and harder. Bobby peeled his face away from Kent's momentarily, looked at his master with tears streaming down his face and heartbreakingly whispered, "I love you Master Kent..." Kent wrapped his arms again around his boy and kissed and kissed him, then whispered in his ear, "I love to too Bobby, I love you so much it hurts boy..."

While Master Kent and his boy were enjoying each other on the couch the leather man's captured cop buddy was now reluctantly sucking Otis' huge manhood. Otis was squatted slightly down and it would have appeared to anyone who happened by that he was using the cop's mouth as a urinal. Tears of fear and shame had welled up in Officer McLaughlin's eyes as he was fed a second helping of huge cock.

"Yeah, that's it Officer, mindless am I?" Otis chuckled. "I may be mindless but you're a real good cock sucker..."

As Otis mouth raped the cop the officer felt his own cock again stiffening between his stretched out legs.

"Holy fucking shit Otis my man, look at this," Cleeve laughed. "The cop is getting a second goddamned hard-on."

Officer McLaughlin tried to ignore the enjoyable sensations his captor was causing as Cleeve took his big sausage in hand and began stroking him. In no time at all the cop's cock was again at full mast, his juicy balls, kiwi-sized wriggled in their sexy sac as Cleeve stroked and choked his manhood. As the cop was being mouth fucked by Otis he arched his hips up and down, grinding his naked ass cheeks against the ground in what seemed a sexual frenzy. As he was forced to slurp and slobber over the cock in his mouth he heard Cleeve announcing mockingly "Looks like the cop is really enjoying the party."

With a loud grunt that was muffled by Otis' cock jammed deep down his throat Officer McLaughlin shot his second load on the ground, feeling totally sleazy and humiliated as Cleeve stroked his mess from him. As he shot his load the cop found himself at the same time swallowing Otis' mess of ball juice. His lips worked double time as he scoffed down the giant guy's rancid tasting slime... The sounds of two men popping their loads filled the sea scented air...

When he managed to gather his thoughts somewhat coherently the cop realized he was totally consumed with rage mixed with shame at having been so thoroughly bested by two lowlifes such as Cleeve and Otis. He was a goddamned cop, a good goddamned cop and a cop of his stature should not have had something so humiliating happen to him. His manly pride had been shattered and as he sat there while the two men stood over him, their cocks dripping remnants of cum and beads of piss he was reduced to pleading.

"Okay guys, you've had your fun the last two days with Bobby and now with me, I've sucked your goddamned cocks," the cop said as pleadingly as possible, knowing that pleading would more than likely be the only way out of this for him. "Now take my cuffs off me and let me go...okay?"

"Let you go Officer Stupid?" Cleeve asked. "Let you go? You got to be kiddin, ha!! We got lots more stuff to teach you cop! Look at this as cop training, the stuff they didn't teach you at the academy! And as the Carpenter's said in that song, we've only just begun."

The cop groaned miserably, wondering just what the fucking fucks they were going to do to him next. He didn't have all that long to wait to find out. The cop's hat, which had fallen off his head when Cleeve had struck him with the lead pipe, was now in Cleeve's hands. The burly guy held the cop's cap and was grinning wickedly.

"I don't know about you Otis, but after I shoot a big load I really have to piss like a racehorse," Cleeve said mockingly.

"I know just what the fuck you mean Cleeve," Otis chortled.

Sitting on the ground bare assed the cop watched as the two men proceeded to use his cap as a toilet, both of them pissing into it.

"Fuckers, how disrespectful is that??? Pissing in a cop's uniform hat???" the officer seethed.

"Wait'll you see what we're gonna do with our piss you idiot cop," Cleeve laughed as his stream and Otis' seemed to go on and on as they piss filled the cap.

When they were done pissing the cop's cap was filled to the

brim with his captor's yellow juices.

"Now look what we cooked up for you cop, straight from our cop mouth spent cocks," Cleeve said, holding the cap in front of the officer's face.

The scent of warm piss assaulted the cop's nostrils and his stomach turned in apprehension. He didn't need three guesses to know what the two men were going to make him do with the piss in his cap.

"Doesn't that look appetizing cop?" Otis asked. "It came from the same place all that goo you ate came from, right from our big cocks."

Officer McLaughlin whimpered miserably...

"Yeah, and now that you've eaten our cum we'll give you a nice face full of piss to wash it all down with, how's that sound?" Cleeve asked the trapped cop.

In response Officer McLaughlin whimpered louder...

The cop then felt Otis' huge hands as they gripped his head, tilting it back. He forced the cop's mouth wide open again. Cleeve did the honors of tilting the hat slowly over the cop's gaping craw. The warm yellow liquid spilled over the bill of the cop's cap and slopped down into his mouth. Each time his mouth was filled Otis pressed the cop's head and chin till his mouth closed and he was forced to chug down the vile tasting piss. The two men repeated this action till all the piss had been fed to the cop, the cop blubbering madly as he drank it down. When he was done Cleeve tossed the sopped hat aside. The cop nearly blanched when Cleeve said "Okay, cop training would not be complete without a little ass fucking." Officer McLaughlin looked at up at Cleeve as he and Otis leered down at him...

Without another word Cleeve grabbed the cop's muscular thighs and hoisted them, yanking them back to raise McLaughlin's ass up off the ground, exposing his rosebud of a shit chute...

"OH NO, no, don't fuck my ass you bastards," the cop blubbered desperately. "Not with those huge cocks you two got...oh GOD, you'll break me in two if..."

But the poor trapped cop's pleadings were cut short as Otis slid his jeans and underpants down and squatted over the cop with his muscular ass on the officer's face. He efficiently fit the raunchy crack of his ass over McLaughlin's nose and placed his stinking asshole directly over the cop's mouth. Otis wiggled his butt and enjoyed the stimulating feeling of the officer's pants against his now open shit chute.

"AAAWWWKKK...mmmffff..." Officer McLaughlin seethed as his tongue seemed to involuntarily start slurping and eating at Otis' hole.

"Oh yeah, that's it you dumb stack of muscled cop, make sweet on my buddy's asshole while I get your shit chute ready back here for some good old fashioned reaming..." the cop heard Cleeve saying and then felt Cleeve pry his asshole open with three fingers.

Officer McLaughlin, a total dominant who never got fucked by anyone twisted miserably as Cleeve's fingers dug deep inside him, as if digging for gold, all the while he had no choice but to keep feasting miserably on Otis's stink hole.

"OHHHH man Cleeve, this cop is really kissin' my damned hole," Otis laughed and meanly farted while the officer did his work.

"GGGGGRRRFFFFFF!!!" the cop seethed as he inhaled the awful fumes.

A short while later Otis was holding the cop by one leg to keep his rosebud exposed while Cleeve positioned himself at the prized opening.

"NO...no...don't fuck me you guys...don't this to me..." the downed officer grunted, the taste of Otis' asshole and the remnants of piss and cum filling his craw as he spoke. "I DO NOT get fucked you lowlifes! I'm a top cop and...YOWWWWWWWWWWW!!!!"

Ignoring the cop's desperate pleas Cleeve drove his un-lubricated huge erection into the tied up cop's asshole, spearing his rosebud from the tip of his cock all the way to his nest of pubic hair. The cop's eyes opened wide as he shrieked in a man's agony, his virgin ass being smashed to smithereens it seemed. It felt to the cop as if Cleeve's jackhammer of a cock was splitting him in two. He fleetingly wondered if Cleeve had fucked poor Bobby this way. He could feel the damned thing pulsing and alive inside him as it stretched his innards, it seemed to reach his shit and the officer felt as if it would slide up and out of his throat. "OHHH GAWD, it hurts you fucker, fucking pile driving me here like I was some cheap whore down at the waterfront," the officer seethed and sobbed.

"Damn Cleeve that looks like its more fun than fucking his mouth was," Otis laughed. "I want to fuck him too..."

"Sure thing Otis my man, this cop hole belongs to us for now and we can do any fucking thing we want with it..." Cleeve panted as he drove his huge manhood deeper and deeper into John's hole with each thrust.

While Officer McLaughlin was feeling that he would die of shame from having had his cherry popped by Cleeve and Otis of all people Master Kent and Bobby were now at headquarters. They were sitting at the missing cop's desk, speaking with Officer Robinson. Robinson, a square jawed ruggedly handsome black cop sat behind John's desk looking intently at Bobby and Master Kent. Even though the leather master had related the story of Bobby's abduction, tortures, and eventual release to him over the phone he and his boy still went through it one more time in person for Officer Robinson. Master Kent sat there trying in earnest to control his rage as Bobby related what had been done to him at the hands and other parts of Cleeve and Otis.

"My God, you poor guy," Officer Robinson said, leaning forward over the desk, basking secretly in Bobby's utter beauty, his hands under his chin. "And now you think that Cleeve and Otis are doing the same thing to Officer McLaughlin that they did to you?"

"I don't know anything for sure," Bobby said. "I only know that they managed to snag him and that they most definitely have him trapped somewhere. Fuck, they won't release him till he's really been worked over. And judging from the size of McLaughlin that won't be for a while, you see, he looks like the sort of cop who can really take it."

"But Kent, you told me that all the other victims had been released after twenty-four hours or so," Robinson said, now looking intently at Kent.

"John is a cop," Master Kent replied. "Bobby and I get the feeling that those two monsters will give him special treatment and hold onto him a little longer than that."

Officer Robinson proceeded to put an APB out on Officer John McLaughlin, even though all three men seated at that desk seemed to know inwardly that it would turn up naught. Officer Robinson then thanked Bobby and Master Kent for coming down to headquarters, shook their hands and the two men left the precinct. As they walked down the steps outside the police station Bobby looked down at the sidewalk, squinted his eyes and rubbed an open palmed hand over his forehead.

"You all right boy?" Kent asked him and placed a steadying hand on his shoulder.

"I want to go home and get some more sleep Master Kent,"

Bobby said, looking at Kent dejectedly. "I'm not feeling too well..."

The two men walked to their car and got in, Kent in the driver's seat. Before starting the car he pulled his boy close to him and hugged him tight. Bobby held equally as tight to Kent as he had back at home and the leather man gently kissed the top of Bobby's head.

"I love you boy, I love you so much," Master Kent said softly but gruffly. "You're going to be okay, I promise."

Bobby pulled away, smiled through the tears in his eyes, and leaned back in the passenger seat as the man he called "Master" Started the car.

A while had passed since Cleeve and Otis had been taking turns fucking their captive cop's asshole. The big handsome officer was now draped ass-up over a fallen garbage pail. At that point he was barely conscious. Cleeve and Otis had fucked all sense from him it seemed. His asshole had been stretched beyond reason and it was dripping slugs upon slugs of the two men's semen as he lay there. As miserable as he was feeling both mentally and physically his two captors continued to use his now unresisting body for their perverse pleasures. Even now Otis was busily chugging his sore but hard cock up the cop's syrupy asshole.

"Fuck it all Cleeve, what do you suppose this cop's buddies would say if they could see him now?" Otis laughed as he meanly plowed away at Officer McLaughlin's hole, holding the cop's ass up by one ankle. "Getting his goddamned shit chute fucked and fucked like it was some pussy..."

"Yeah, shame on you Officer Stupid," Cleeve chuckled as the cop's head spun in a reverse orbit. "Fucking stupid cop, letting yourself get captured, tied up and raped by a couple of big guys..."

Otis grunted in a man's primal sounding passion as he slid his cock as deep as possible in the semiconscious cop's rear end...

"Well, believe it or not Otis my man, that's it for me...I'm callin' it quits for now," Cleeve mused. "My nuts are truly drained dry. What with fucking that master's sweet boy and now this hunky cop...FUCK!!!"

"Fuck is right Cleeve, you screwed the cop six times over," Otis said in amazement. "This is only my fifth time and I'm ready to give it a rest myself..."

"OOOHHHHH GOD," Officer McLaughlin groaned more to himself than to the two men that had captured him. "My asshole, my poor, poor asshole, these monsters have turned it into a slimy pussy..."

The cop looked up from his position over the garbage pail and saw Cleeve sitting against a wall. Thick sloppy remnants of cum and shit were all over the huge guy's flaccid cock. As he looked at Cleeve's cock Otis grunted that he was cumming yet again. As he filled the cop's chute with his sticky juices he meanly swatted and spanked the officer's ass cheeks...

By the time Cleeve and Otis had finished fucking the poor cop he was whimpering and crying like a baby. He tried to crawl away from the two men that had captured him, his hands no longer locked in his own cuffs at that point. But as he tried to make an escape crawling Cleeve grabbed one of his socked ankles and dragged him back like he was a huge rag doll.

"Where you going cop?" Cleeve teased the poor officer. "We are far from finished with you..."

At that point Officer John McLaughlin totally lost consciousness. With all that he had been through it was amazing he had managed to stay awake for all of it...

As the cop lay on the concrete Cleeve said, "I know a way that we can really put that cunt hole of his to some good use and make us some extra spending bucks at the same time," and he began writing some lettering on a piece of cardboard that he'd found. In large letters Cleeve wrote, "FUCK THE COP...$3.00... BLOW JOB...$1.00

The two men packed their spent cocks into their jeans and Otis picked up the unconscious cop, slinging him over a shoulder. He followed Cleeve down the deserted area of the sleazy waterfront.

"Where are we taking him Cleeve?" Otis asked.

"Ha, where we're takin' him there are a bunch of horny guys who would just love to have a shot or two or three at that juicy cunt hole we made," Cleeve laughed, walking in front of Otis.

"You mean "The Local?" Otis asked.

"You got it," Cleeve said as they then headed for their infamous van...

When Master Kent and Bobby got home Bobby went straight to their bedroom, stripped down to his underpants and stretched out on the bed. After he had been asleep for a good while Kent decided to check in on him. He silently opened the door and seeing his boy lying there peacefully asleep yet troubled stole the leather master's heart. He sat down on a chair that they kept next to the bed, (a chair that many times Bobby found himself tightly tied to during some of Master

Kent's endurance tests) and just sat there staring at the boy, sort of the way a father will look at his new born baby through the glass in a maternity ward in a hospital. What John had said was so true Master Kent thought. He was so lucky to have such a handsome boy who was so totally devoted to him. Kent watched as Bobby's chest moved up and down as he breathed softly in his sleep, lying there on his side. He would do anything for this boy, the leather master said to himself; he was that great, he was so wonderful. The leather master thought how Bobby was very kind-hearted, how the boy would do anything for a friend at any time. Master Kent seethed then as he looked over Bobby's bruises and scrapes, how those two monsters Cleeve and Otis had hurt him in ways that the leather man could not even imagine. To Kent it didn't even bear thinking about. He leaned forward and looked intently at his handsome boy's sleeping face and at that moment he swore that he would someday make Cleeve and Otis pay for what they had done to Bobby. As he leaned back in the chair it creaked slightly and Bobby's eyes opened. At the sight of Master Kent he smiled warmly.

"Sir, how long have you been sitting there?" Bobby asked.

"A few minutes," Kent replied. "I just wanted to be with you."

Bobby reached out a hand, whispered the word "Sir" and took Master Kent's hand in his.

"I love you Master Kent, Sir," Bobby whispered.

The leather man's heart thundered in his chest. He got out of the chair and lay down next to his boy. He gathered Bobby into his arms, kissed his neck, his eyes, his earlobes and hugged and hugged and hugged him, Bobby loving his master more each second as he hugged him back.

"I love you Bobby, never forget that boy," Master Kent said and pressed his mouth down on Bobby's.

The two men lay there like that for quite a while, simply holding each other. Bobby didn't seem to want to let go of Master Kent and the rugged leather man had no problem with that. Kent smiled as he thought how he could hold onto Bobby for the rest of their lives together, and he intended to do just that...

By late afternoon the seedy bar known as "The Local" is always filled with a hard-drinking and rowdy crowd of sleazy and depraved men. It's the same bar where the handsome sailor, Petty Officer Jack Higgins unwittingly found himself tied up to a stall door in the men's room with his unusually large and hard cock sticking out of the glory hole cut in that stall door for all the cock suckers at the bar to have at that night. **(From the story "Milked Sailor.")** That poor sailor shot his load more times that night than on any time he had been stationed by the navy in different cities and found himself in the arms of cheap female whores. By the time Petty Officer Jack Higgins stumbled exhausted and overly spent from the bar at 4:00 AM his balls had been milked drier than an old man's flaky skin. "The Local" is also the bar where handsome and muscular bank executive "Greg Smith" found himself to be tied up in the same stall as Sailor boy Jack Higgins, in the same circumstances, being milked and sucked dry over and over again. But to the sailor's one time being trapped in that stinking stall Greg Smith had lost count of how many times the two bar owners had gotten the drop on him, stripped him of his suit and roped him to that stall door for an all night milking session. **(From the story "Greg Smith- The Times of My Life.)** Now, while the sleazy and sordid men that regularly frequented "The Local" filled the place to just about full capacity they were all very happily and sadistically surprised when Cleeve and Otis arrived, dragging between them the limp, and unconscious Officer John McLaughlin. A few of the guys at the bar recognized the handsome hard-nosed officer from nights when they'd had too much to drink and he had pulled them over and issued them pricey tickets. Smiling evilly they realized very quickly how this was their chance to make due and to get even with the ruggedly handsome and muscular officer of the law. The cop's already overly fucked asshole was still gaping and wide open, soaked, dripping and leaking cum. On the ride from the waterfront to "The Local" the cop had screamed and passed out yet again in the van when Otis decided to fist him. When the crowd at "The Local" saw the sign that Cleeve held up the entire bar erupted into loud jeers, and whoops of rough laughter. The cop groaned miserably as he was dragged into the whiskey smelling establishment, his socked toes dragging on the hardwood floor, him having been de-shoed in the van on the way over... All that the cop wore at that point were his knee length navy blue dress socks and the tattered remains of his uniform shirt... His flaccid cock swung dangling between his tree trunks like thighs as the two men entered the bar with him...

"Hey you guys check this out," Cleeve called out to the assembled crowd. "Me and my buddy Otis are selling this cop's juicy ass real cheap for some hardcore fucking! Any of you sleazes interested?"

As Cleeve made his announcement no one in the bar was aware of how he was sizing up a few of the more muscular guys, possibilities for future marks for him and Otis. From what seemed like far away Officer McLaughlin heard Cleeve making his declaration and the poor cop surmised very quickly (in his stupor state of mind) that his poor ass was in for another mean workout, and this time it would be even more grueling than what Cleeve and Otis had already done to it. It was only the late afternoon and the cop knew that what Cleeve had called his training was about to be taken a few levels higher. Only the afternoon, but somehow Officer McLaughlin knew that he would be a prisoner at "The Local" till the late night and into the early morning hours, what he sometimes referred to as the wee hours of the morning. Cleeve and Otis hoisted the battered cop face-up onto the pool table that dominated the epicenter of the sleazy bar. They each grabbed one of his socked ankles and raised his muscular legs up overhead to really put on display the abused asshole to the overly horned up crowd.

"Holy fuck and I use the term loosely," one of the guys exclaimed. "That cop's hole looks like it's been to hell..."

"Sure as shit and I use that term loosely," Cleeve responded. "But take our word for it Mister; there are still a lot of good fucks left in it..."

"Ohhhrrrr, wha-what...where...where the fuck am I?" the cop suddenly groaned throatily as he slowly came to, taking in the sight of all the men who were inspecting his asshole as he lay atop the pool table with his legs up in the air like some two-bit whore.

"Why, you're on a pool table Offisair," a burly, hugely muscled black guy with no shirt on replied to Officer McLaughlin. "And you're about to be gang fucked like nobody's goddamned business, sheeeei-itttt!!!"

Several of the guys were meanly probing and digging their fingers into the cop's asshole, squeezing his hindquarters as his delectable tight buns dangled off the edge of the pool table. His ass he thought miserably, his poor ass, it had been violated and used. The cop had always prided himself on being a total top man. No one and that meant no one ever fucked him. Now it had been deflowered and worse yet, it belonged at the moment to any one of these guy's who chose to shove whatever the fuck they decided on into it.

"This is it gentlemen," Otis chortled, pointing at the cop's ass. "Let's get this party started, right!!"

"Let's warm this fucking cop up first," a guy wearing a cowboy hat suggested. "I remember this officer of the law well, fucking guy ticketed me twice! "Fucking fuck man, but that hole of his is going to be shredded to mince meat by the time we're all done here. I got just the thing to fix it so he'll actually enjoy what we're going to do to him..."

As they flipped John over onto his belly he was suddenly fully alert, but helpless nonetheless as a funnel was inserted into his butt hole.

"You guys would do well to release me now and... ULLLPPPPPPP!!!" John blubbered as a bottle of tequila was poured through the funnel wedged in his sopped hole.

The helpless cop felt the searing liquor being poured into his rectal hole and the warmth spread quickly through his belly and crotch areas in a somewhat pleasant way. As a second bottle of liquor was poured into his asshole the cop had difficulty focusing and his head spun away yet again. He stupidly thought, "What a day this turned out to be..." From somewhere far away Officer McLaughlin heard the guy wearing the cowboy hat say, "Drink up Officer, that tequila will really put you in a partying mood..."

And then, to the captured officer's dismay (and possibly his delight) the all afternoon and all night fucking began.

"And let the games begin!" the guy wearing the cowboy hat said as he mounted the pool table and dangled his nine inch cock over the cop's trembling lips while a buddy of his took position at the officer's exposed rosebud, holding his thighs straight up.

The crowd of rowdy men used the poor cop mercilessly. Sometimes, like the guy wearing the cowboy hat and his buddy they used him two at a time, one guy feeding his mouth hard cock while another rammed his asshole with concrete hard man-meat. The would-be rapists lined up, set down their monies and took what they paid for. A certain well-built and handsome construction worker who reminded Cleeve somewhat of Bobby caught the serial kidnapper's eye. When Cleeve smiled at him the young guy had no clue as to what was going through Cleeve's evil imagination. For Officer McLaughlin the late afternoon became a blur of horny cocks and what seemed like gallons of jazz as he sucked and swallowed and had his ass fucked and soaked.

"I'm next," a well muscled black guy bellowed.

"Quit shoving Tyrone," the handsome construction worker who

Cleeve had eyed said to the black guy. "I was ahead of you and I plan to fuck that cop six ways to Sunday, hardy, har, har!!"

"Oh man, I cannot wait to pork that cop's ass," a bearded raunchy guy drawled in a drunken stupor.

"I'm going for his mouth, look at how those sweet lips of his curl around cock," another guy in the line said as they watched the cop sucking off one of their buddies.

"OOOHHHHHH...b-bastards," Officer McLaughlin panted at one point while his mouth was not being used. "Y-you're all under arrest...es-especially those two monsters that brought me here collecting your money...MMMMFFFFFFFF!!!!"

The crowd laughed and another guy quickly filled the cop's craw to keep him quiet...

As the afternoon turned to evening the sex-crazed crowd became evilly creative in their rapes of the cop and more than just cocks were then used on the liquor-drugged officer. At one point John felt something cold and unyielding pressing against his poor ass cheeks. Good God, the cop thought, they were shoving the neck of an empty wine bottle up his poor shit chute. He tried to clench his ass cheeks shut, to somehow keep the glass invasion from entering his rear end. But the liquor they'd poured into his ass seemed to have wiped away all his resistance. With no choice in the matter the cop spread his muscular thighs, arched his back as he now lay on the floor, belly up on his palms and he felt the wine bottle slide in. The cold glassy length of it brought an erotic tingle to his innards. As the guy shoving the bottle in gloated meanly he twisted it around inside the cop's chute, making him moan in a mixture of misery and what was somehow sounding like ecstasy. A guy who looked like a cross between a motorcycle hood and a wrestler stepped in front of John as he lay there with his upper body raised on the palms of his hands. The biker type dropped his jeans halfway down and presented a stinking butt to the delirious cop.

"Ain't my ass pretty?" the biker grunted. "If you want to eat it out I won't stop you."

The cop knew that this was more a demand than a request that the biker was making of him. The terrified officer obediently stuck out his tongue and began to lap hungrily at the hairy and stinking rosebud. The awful taste of it was rancid on the cop's tongue but as the guy at his ass shoved the wine bottle deeper inside him Officer McLaughlin found himself going to town as he sucked at the biker's asshole, making loud slurping sounds, which sent the crowd of rapists into a hysterical laughing jag. The poor cop was mystified with himself as he dug his tongue deeper and deeper into the guy's anal canal, tasting the guy's moistness back there and swallowing his ass chowder hungrily. All the while the other guy busily fucked the cop's ass with the neck of the wine bottle, shoving it in further yet, inch by awful inch till only part of the bottle's base was visible...

"OOOOHHHHHHHHH FUCKING FUCK..." the cop groaned loudly.

"Shhhhheeeit," the muscular black guy laughed. "This cop's got one hungry asshole here. Just look how easy that bottle slid in..."
As the cop licked and sucked the biker's shit chute he stuck his butt up in the air, like a bitch in heat, the short green bottle sticking out of his most private area rather obscenely. The peals of laughter in the bar grew louder and to a higher crescendo...

While the afternoon wore on and while Officer McLaughlin was being used as a sex toy for the crowd of depraved men at "The Local" Master Kent and Bobby were now downstairs in the leather man's dungeon. The dungeon was actually the basement of the house, which Master Kent had had transformed and properly outfitted as an erotic torture chamber of sorts. Kent was clad in a pair of black leather engineer boots, black leather shorts and a black leather vest. Bobby stood before him wearing just his frosty white briefs and a black silk blindfold tied over his eyes. The boy's hands were tightly tied behind him and his cock was hanging out of his underpants, long, beefy and hard.

"Are you sure you're up to this Bobby?" Master Kent asked his boy, holding him tightly from behind, his big strong arms wrapped tightly around the kid, his lips grazing the back of his boy's neck.

"Yes Master Kent, oh yes, please, please make me service you properly Sir, I missed you so much while those two bastards had me trapped," Bobby whispered breathlessly, sounding more like he was whispering in ecstasy and fear at the same time, the two things that really set the boy in motion. *"I need you Master Kent."*

The leather man let go of his boy and leaned up against a post in the middle of the large room.

"Okay Bobby, I'm waiting for you," Kent said to him as softly as possible, not wanting the boy to know exactly where in the room he was.

Bobby followed the sound of his master's soft-spoken voice

and made his way slowly over to him. It was a game that Master Kent had invented for them back when they had first met. Actually, it was one of many games that the leather man had invented for the purposes of training his boy. In this particular game, if Bobby found Master Kent without a problem the boy earned the privilege of servicing his master's tits, cock, feet and whatever other parts of the well-muscled leather man he was hungry for at that moment. However, if the boy did not find his master in the allotted time the leather man got to whip Bobby's beautiful ass pretty harshly. Many times over the boy had learned a lesson the hard way, being ass whipped pretty severely by his master. Bobby always thanked his master for it though and promised to do better next time. This time Master Kent would let the kid find him if he had to. No way was the leather man going to be beating the poor kid's ass at the moment, not after all he had recently been through. More than anything Master Kent knew that Bobby really needed his attention that day. With a grin on his handsome blindfolded face Bobby made his way slowly and carefully over to the man he called "Master", listening intently for the sounds of his breathing, sniffing for the wonderful scent of leather. When he was inches from Master Kent he stuck out his tongue and flicked it around a few times until he found one of the leather man's exposed nipples.

"Found you Master Kent," Bobby said, sounding proud of himself as he gave the hard nipple a few hearty licks and slurps.

Master Kent pressed a hand against the back of Bobby's neck and held him tight as the boy alternately serviced his nipples expertly, knowing just how his master wanted it done, knowing full well how to satisfy the master who loved him dearly. Bobby pressed his face against Master Kent's hugely muscular chest and Kent gave the boy's beautiful butt cheeks a hard squeeze through his frosty white briefs, loving the feel of them, kneading them. As Bobby moved down toward Kent's hard cock in his leather shorts the leather master was beyond proud of his boy at that moment. Cleeve and Otis had not ruined Bobby's appetite for sex, training or for the kinky games that he and Master Kent acted out. Master Kent knew that Bobby was stronger than those two monsters ever knew. Now, on his knees in front of his master Bobby leaned over and kissed the tops of Kent's boots. Master Kent's heart swelled (and so did his cock) with more than love for the boy at that moment...

"Ohhhhhhrrrrr..." Officer John McLaughlin bellowed as one of

So, laughing meanly ten guys crowded around the cop's asshole and took turns shoving their fists up into his asshole, grabbed one of the balls inside him and yanked it out. Each time a ball was yanked out the cop screeched. Each guy would check the number printed on the ball he had just retrieved. To better see the number the cop was made to lick the slimy ass juices off the balls. By then his mouth was a rancid spittoon tasting of piss, cum, man-sweat and now his own ass sap. When all ten balls had been taken out of the cop's ass the scores were noted for that round, then, to the cop's horror the men reinserted the balls one by one for the next round.

"OHHHHHHH MY GAWD!!!! OH MY FUCKS!!!! OHHHHH NO YOU MONSTERS!!" the cop gurgled and by now was struggling in his captor's grasps as they again packed his shit chute with billiard balls.

By the time the game was over the poor cop's asshole had been packed and emptied nearly a dozen times. Cleeve did the honors of adding up the men's scores and the huge cocked soldier on leave who had won the free fuck took his "prize" right there on the billiard table. As the soldier dropped his fatigue pants and inserted his pounding cock into the cop's asshole Cleeve eyed the soldier boy lecherously, thinking what a great mark he would make for him and Otis.

Much Later…

By the time the night was nearly over and the sound of "Last Call" was heard being bellowed from the bar, Officer John McLaughlin's asshole had been rudely fucked to what felt like pulp. His mouth seemed to be permanently locked into an open circle as he sucked cock after cock after cock. He felt that it would be weeks before he was able to walk properly or close up his poor butt hole. His socks were dangling half off his feet and the tattered remains of his uniform shirt hung off his muscular torso. He was slathered in cum and piss and he stunk to the highest heavens but his ravishers didn't seem to care or notice. They still went on plunking down their money so that they could pound away at his openings, ramming cocks, fists, dildos and bottles up his poor ruined ass. As the words "Last Call" was announced for the last time Cleeve and Otis counted the money they had collected from selling the cop's ass and mouth like he was a whore. It actually amounted to a very sizeable sum of cash. Cleeve and Otis snickered meanly a while later when they exited the bar, taking the cop with them…

Part Three
The Night when Master Kent First met Bobby
(as told by Master Kent himself)
(1985)

It had been two days now that my buddy Officer John McLaughlin was missing, still in the clutches of those two monsters Cleeve and Otis. It really made me ache inside, first my boy Bobby had suffered horribly at their hands when they had captured him and now my good buddy, John. From what we knew of Cleeve and Otis they only held onto their victims for a maximum of twenty-four hours. My buddy John seemed to be a different story for them. (Other victims of Cleeve and Otis, the ones that reported their abductions and abuse that is, did report being held even longer than a couple of days. One young guy who will have to remain nameless reported that Cleeve and Otis had held him as a sort of sex slave for three weeks. After a while the guy had lost track of the time and only became aware of his captivity having lasted three weeks when he saw the date on the newspaper on the day he was set free. The guy was pretty much a loner and wasn't all that close to anyone. He didn't have much family either, hence the reasons that no one reported him missing all that time. The guy did say though that being held prisoner by Cleeve and Otis had cost him his job. He did not want his boss knowing that he'd been kidnapped and used in the way he had been.) But now, having a bad motherfucker of a cop like my buddy Officer John McLaughlin in their grasp must have been just too much of a treat for the two psychos to handle. John is built like a mountain and he can take whatever the fuck is dished out on him, hence the reason those two bastards still hadn't let him go two days later. The APB that Officer Robinson had put out had not turned up one iota of a clue. God only knew what horrors my good buddy was enduring at the hands of those two sadistic fucks. After what they had done to my boy Bobby I didn't doubt for a second that my poor cop buddy was being brutally tortured as well. And probably worse than in the ways that they had worked Bobby over. I felt as if those two bastards were somehow out to get me through my best buddy and my boy. Bobby had returned to work and as I sat there in the living room holding the framed picture of him I prayed to God to keep him safe. After what Cleeve and Otis had done to him it amazed me that he wanted to return to work in such a short time. But, as always, Bobby insisted that his job as a construction worker kept him fit, trim and strong. Also, he added that he had to get back into the routine of his life and try to put the horrible event that had occurred behind him. If he didn't do it now he insisted he wouldn't be able to later on. I hugged him tightly, kissed the top of his head and held him close to me before he left the house that morning. God, every time I hold him in my arms I never want to let go of him. I could hold onto Bobby for a hundred years and it would not be enough. He told me he would call during his lunch break to see if there was any word on my missing cop buddy. I told him to meet me at the leather bar that I owned after he got off work that night. For whatever the reason I wanted my boy with me at the bar that night. Looking at the picture of him I quickly realized why I wanted him there with me. Pride; pride in the extremely handsome and devoted boy that I had been blessed with. As stated in the last two testaments, I consider myself beyond lucky to have such a handsome, devoted, rugged, kind hearted and loving slave boy. Every thing Bobby does is with thoughts of pleasing me in mind. Even with his job as a construction worker he works hard to keep his body strong and muscular for what I put him through, endless tests of his strength and endurance. It seems that there is nothing that I can put Bobby through that he won't take. *And he takes it all,* knowing how very much I love him, how I would die for him. From the moment we met he was devoted to me. We were instantly comfortable with each other; it was as if we had known each other in a past life. No matter how I treated him he would always take it, knowing that I only meant to strengthen him even more. Even on the night we met when I was treating him gruffly, meanly and sternly I think he sensed then and there my overpowering love for him. Sitting there, looking at his picture I thought of the night at the leather bar that I own when I first met him. Had two years really gone by that quickly? Had it been two years already that I was so blessed? So blessed yet those two monsters Cleeve and Otis almost caused me to lose it all when they abducted my boy and tortured the living fuck out of him. And for no reason it seemed except that it got them their jollies to torture and torment innocent men like Bobby. It made me wonder what could have happened to two men to make them that way. But even they could not break my boy's resolve and devotion to me. God, I can kill those two monsters for what they did to him. Two years I thought as I ran the tip of my finger over Bobby's smiling face in the picture frame...

It had been a night like any other at the hard-core leather bar that I own in the city. It was eleven PM and the place was just starting to get crowded. Masters searching for slave boys, slave boys searching for masters and some masters there with their slave boys in tow. Some of the masters even had their slave boys on leashes as they walked through the bar. The bar I own has two levels. On the ground floor there are two bars and a pool table in the center of the place. In the back are the restrooms. I have a shoe and boot polishing stand set up in a corner for masters who desire their slaves to tongue clean their boots for them. The second level of the bar is quieter than the bottom. There are tables set up with chairs where masters and their boys can sit and talk, the slave boys tied or leashed to the chairs of course. Or perhaps masters only where they can discuss better ways of keeping their boys in line. As I said the place was pretty crowded. Some of the guys I recognized and greeted by name. They shook my hand and returned polite greetings addressing me as "Master Kent." My friend Master Jeff had his slave boy Chris greet me by squatting and leaning down to kiss my boots. I told Master Jeff that he had trained his boy very well.

"Thank you Kent, that's a nice compliment coming from you," Master Jeff said and took a sip of his beer.

His slave boy Chris was still on his knees between us. He would not stand up until his master gave him permission to do so. I had to respect that.

"So tell me Kent, when are you going to find a boy all your own?" Master Jeff asked me. "For as long as I've known you you've been single."

"I don't know man," I replied, not knowing what fate had in store for me that very night. "Someday I suppose. Good to see you Master Jeff."

Smiling, I walked away from Master Jeff and moved slowly through the getting crowded bar. I really had no desire to listen to anymore of Master Jeff's prattle about my being single. The scent of raw man sweat, leather and whiskey filled the air erotically in the dimly lit bar. God, I was proud of this place. It was nothing like that dive called "The Local" down by the waterfront. Mine was a respectable more upscale bar that was for sure. *And Master Jeff was right.* I had been single too long. Whether I wanted to listen to him or not the man was right. I did want a slave boy, but not just a part time slave. I wanted a relationship. I wanted someone to share all this with. I had worked hard to make the bar a success. At the age of thirty three I was beyond successful. I had spent my twenties getting this place off the ground and now it was done. I had a thriving business, but no one to share it with. I wanted someone that I could love and someone who would return that love, loving each other in the special ways that leather men do. As I said I had no idea what fate had in mind for me that night. Craig was tending bar at the left-hand and Steve was on duty at the right-hand bar. Craig is a five foot nine guy with wavy black hair and deep dark eyes. His body is on the lanky side and because of his lankiness he looked superb in his tight fitting tank top and leather pants as he tended bar. Steve is a burly five foot seven guy with short cropped brown hair, ala military style and intense green eyes. He is extremely muscular from the workouts he punishes himself through at the gym on a daily basis. Steve always serves bare-chested, his massive chest and pecs on total display, earning him bigger tips from the patrons I would think, and it also earns him some good tit squeezes from the patrons as well. Craig and Steve were both busy serving drinks to countless customers, not missing a beat when orders for beer, shots and hard liquor were shouted to them above the music blaring through the speakers hooked up over the bars. Yeah, a great fucking place my bar was. Friends of mine told me how they had met their master or their boy at my place. I was proud to be able to say that my place helped to form those beautiful trusting relationships that not many people understood. I walked through to the end of the bottom level and turned to head up to the upper level to sit alone with a cold beer. That was how I spent most nights at my bar. Dressed in black leather pants, black engineer boots a black leather vest and a biker's hat I walked slowly back the way I had just come. It was as I passed the end of the right-hand bar that I saw him. He was sitting at the far end of the bar sipping a Coors light beer. He was chatting with the guy who was sitting next to him and the three guys who were standing around them. For a moment I thought my heart had stopped. He was beyond handsome he was out-rightly beautiful. Our eyes met for about all of three seconds and I swear that I felt tears welling up in my eyes. He was that beautiful. He looked to be about twenty or twenty-one years old. Never before had a guy's face made me want to cry. And for a leather master of my caliber to admit to that it had to be something way beyond special, because as I said, he was beautiful. As stated our eyes met for all of three seconds or so, but for both of us it seemed an eternity. I slowly made my way behind the bar and over to Steve. I again glanced at the handsome kid sitting there with his friends. He was smiling at something that one of his friends had just said. His smile was that of an angel, it lit up his entire face. We again stole glances at each other and then looked away from each other. At the sight of me behind the bar Steve was instantly at my beck and call. I whispered some instructions to him and slowly walked off, headed for the upper level of the bar, taking a cold beer with me. Steve walked over to the handsome young man at the end of the bar and leaned down close to him.

"Excuse me," Steve said to him. "I'm Steve; may I ask your name?"

The young man looked at his four buddies and then turned his attention to Steve.

"I'm Robert, but my buddies all call me Bobby," the young man replied with a beguiling smile. "What can I do for you Steve?"

"The owner of the bar asked me to give you a drink on the house, anything you want," Steve said to Bobby. "That's him headed up the stairs over there."

Bobby and his friends turned to look and saw me walking slowly up the steps to the second level.

He also said to please extend an invitation for you to join him up there for that drink," Steve went on. "If you're not already committed to someone else already..."

That said Steve looked at the guys Bobby was with, an awkward and quizzical expression on his face.

"Uh, no, we're all just good buddies here, he, he wants *me* to join him?" Bobby said in disbelief. *"Why me?"*

"I don't know; why don't you find out?" Steve asked Bobby with a grin. "I've been working for Master Kent for a long while now and I can honestly say that he has never asked anyone to join him for a drink, let alone to treat them to a drink. You must seem really special to him."

Bobby gulped and looked at his buddy sitting next to him.

"Go ahead Bobby," his buddy sitting next to him said and his other friends' nodded agreement as well.

"That fucking leather master is a hunk Bobby, go on, join him for a beer," another of Bobby's friends said encouragingly.

By now I was seated at my favorite table overlooking the lower area of the bar, watching the conversation transpire between Steve and Bobby. Would he join me? My heart raced with the anticipation.

"O-okay," Bobby said nervously. "Thanks Steve, I'll have a Coors light."

Steve placed a fresh bottle in front of Bobby. The boy tipped him, picked up the bottle and slowly headed for the stairs. One of Bobby's buddies who had been standing sat down on the stool he had just vacated and Steve resumed serving other patrons. With a pensive look on his beautiful face Bobby came up the stairs and over to the table I was seated at. As I said the upper level of the bar is much quieter than the lower level is, making it easy for two people to have a conversation. It is also like the lower level in that it is dimly lit. A small, lit candle adorns the center of each table. Bobby stopped walking when he'd reached my table. He seemed erotically nervous, yet somehow I knew that he knew what I wanted, what we both wanted.

"Good evening," I said to him, holding up my bottle of beer and taking a sip of it.

"Good evening Sir," Bobby said to me. "Thank you for the beer Sir."

"You're more than welcome boy," I replied, noticing that he had not yet sat down across from me.

Obviously he was awaiting my permission. I liked that the boy had respect. He was dressed in mustard colored calf length scuffed work boots black jeans tucked down into those boots and a tight fitting white tee shirt. He was sweating a little and the tips of his nipples were poking against his tee shirt. I could also tell from the way his tee shirt outlined his torso that he was well muscled and nicely toned. Looking at him with a stern sneer my heart accelerated in my chest. Just looking at him stole my breath.

"What's your name boy?" I asked him, sounding a little gruff.

"Sir, my name is Robert, but my buddies all call me Bobby," he replied with the utmost respect and took a sip of his beer.

The way he was calling me "Sir" sent chills through me. He sounded totally submissive yet totally sure of himself.

"I'm Kent," I said, holding out my hand. "*But* my buddies call me Master Kent. As I think the bartender told you, I own this place."

"Sir, it's a pleasure to meet you Master Kent Sir," Bobby said and reached to shake my hand. "And yes Sir, Steve told me that you are the owner of the bar."

I took his hand in a firm grip and held it for a few seconds longer than was necessary. His palm was sweaty against mine and slightly trembling. His hand was big and meaty yet mine still sort of dwarfed it as we shook.

"Are you nervous about something Bobby?" I asked him, giving his hand a tighter squeeze and rubbing my thumb against the side of it.

"Sir, n-no Sir," he replied with a smile, trying not too successfully to hide the fact that he was indeed nervous.

I let go of his hand.

"Would you like to join me?" I asked him, indicating the seat opposite me.

"Yes, thank you Sir," Bobby said and sat down.

I sat there looking at him for a few long seconds, drinking in the sight of him, wanting to engrave his beautiful face in my memory in case I never saw him again. At that moment I didn't know that I would be spending the rest of my life with this beguiling young man.

"Sir, is, is anything wrong?" Bobby asked me, looking at me apprehensively as I drank him in with my eyes.

"I don't usually sit with anyone up here Bobby," I said to him. "But I have to say that *you* are by far the most magnificent looking young man to ever grace my bar."

"Thank you Sir," Bobby said, almost blushing.

"Who are you here with boy?" I asked him boldly, glancing down at his buddies at the bar.

"A few of my work buddies Sir," Bobby said with a humble smile, inwardly knowing that I was trying to find out if he was in a relationship with anyone. "We all worked late at a job-site and we had heard of this place, so we decided to check it out. We figured being that we were dressed in our construction clothes we would not have a problem getting in. I read where you maintain a rugged dress code for your bar Sir."

I nodded and we both sipped our beers.

"What construction company do you work for boy?" I asked him with authority in my voice.

I wanted to test the waters here, calling him "boy", see if my gruffness would scare him off or just draw him in.

"Sir, I work for Green and Sons," Bobby said. "I'm a crew super-visor, one of the youngest supervisors ever on the job."

He was not scared of my gruffness; instead he seemed to be thriving on it. The way he was holding his beer bottle with two hands around it seemed to attest to that. I sensed that he had a need for what I could give him.

"I've heard of that company," I said to him. "In fact I'm friendly with some of the guys in the higher ups. Good company."

"I agree Sir," Bobby said, looking at me in awe. "My job pays well and at the same time keeps me in very good shape Sir."

He smiled across at me and I think it was at that moment that I knew I loved him. My God, I loved him so much at that moment and would for the rest of my life. I decided then and there that if he would have me as his master I would do *anything* to make him happy. Of course he would have to abide by my rules at the same time. He took another sip of his beer, licked his lips and a chill crept up my spine.

"How old are you boy?" I asked him meanly.

"I'm twenty Sir," Bobby replied and placed his hands flat on the table, a signal of acquiescence's.

Looking at me in a mixture of awe and fear he seemed to be shaking.

"Are you okay Bobby?" I asked him, placing my hand over one of his and squeezing it tight.

"I-I'm not sure Sir," he replied, looking down at my hand over his.

"Look at me!" I suddenly blurted, not letting go of his hand.

His eyes darted up and instantly found mine. We drank in the sight of each other this time. I squeezed his hand tighter.

"I would never hurt you Bobby, unless you submitted to me of course for training purposes," I said to him, still squeezing his hand tight but gen-tly. "And even then it would be for you to please me and to test yourself in the most profound ways imaginable. Do you understand what I mean?"

"I-I think so Sir," Bobby responded shakily, his eyes looking away from me.

"Look at me I said!!" I blurted at him again, squeezing his hand tighter now, inflicting a little pain.

He looked back into my eyes again, a look of pain showing in his eyes. It made him all the more beautiful.

"When I say you can look away from me is when you will look away," I said with total authority. *"Do you understand?"*

"Yes Sir," Bobby replied. "Oh, yes Sir."

My heart swelled with love for this young man and I think by then he knew it, which was why he hadn't gotten up and walked away from me. He was hungry and in need of a good disciplinarian AKA a master.

"So, what brought you to my leather bar tonight?" I asked him, pulling his hand closer toward me, making him lean nearer to me.

The scent of his long hard workday wafted to me and I inhaled it deeply. He was a kid in so many ways but he smelled like a man, a man who had worked hard all day.

"I-I told you Sir, we had heard of this place and," Bobby began.

"What did you hear about it boy?" I asked him, moving my face closer to his.

"Sir, we heard that it was a real cool leather bar where, where a guy, I mean, where a boy could possibly meet a master," Bobby replied through his trembling lips, his lips very close to mine at that point.

A place where a boy could meet a master that was what he said. My God, was I about to become one of the stories that other guys had told me of how they met their slave boy or their master at my bar? Was my bar graced somehow with the divine power of bringing together these very special types of relationships?

"Oh God Bobby," I whispered huskily and pressed my lips against his beautiful pouting ones.

Holding his hand less tightly (not wanting to hurt him) we kissed passionately, hard, yet lovingly on the lips, the taste of our beer mixing with our saliva. Our tongues explored each other's mouth. When we stopped kissing I put a hand behind Bobby's neck and stroked it gently.

"Oh God Bobby," I whispered again, loving the way his name sounded as I spoke it, my lips now grazing his roughly. "I swear, when I saw you boy it took my breath away."

"M-mine too Sir," he said and I placed a finger under his chin, pressing lightly.

His eyes were filled and glistening. I kissed his cheek, keeping my lips pressed lovingly against his face. My goatee rubbed against his smooth cheek and I could feel him tingling. I kissed his beautiful face again and again. My God, I could kiss him a thousand times in a row and it would not be enough. When I let go of him he sat back in his chair and took a long gulp of his beer.

"Do you want another beer?" I asked him.

"I-I'm fine Sir, thank you," he replied.

As he sat there leaning back in his chair I took in his buzz-cut light brown hair, his piercing dark eyes and his smooth square jawed line. He kept looking at me as I had instructed him to do, not taking his eyes off me.

"What's on your mind boy?" I asked him.

Sir, I'm not sure," he said to me. "I mean I came here for a couple of beers and look what's happened. It's kind of overwhelming Master Kent Sir. And yet, I feel somehow that I have finally arrived. Sir, does that make sense at all?"

I held up a finger and gestured for him to move closer to me. He instantly did as he was told. I hadn't even had to use words that time to have him do my bidding. The boy was learning already. I leaned in close, hooked a hand roughly this time around the back of his neck and we kissed again on the mouths, hard and much more ruggedly this time. Bobby's fingers toyed with my thick goatee. I sucked his lips and tongue hard, inflicting pain this time. He took it all, not pleading for me to stop hurting him, already making me proud. When we stopped kissing I looked at him meanly and pointed at the floor next to me.

"Sir?" he asked me, obviously confused.

"Knees," I said to him. "Now! Your training will begin here tonight! As you said boy, you feel as if you've arrived but it doesn't make sense to you. I am going to show you how to make sense of it all. When I point at the floor you will automatically drop to your knees! After tonight you won't need me to say the word. When you see me point you will simply do it. *But for now, knees!"*
With no hesitation Bobby moved out of his seat and knelt on the floor next to my seat.

"That's good boy, that's real fucking good," I said to him. "Head down."

Bobby looked down at my boots and licked his lips hungrily.

"What are you thinking about now boy?" I asked him.

"Sir, my only thoughts are on how to please you," Bobby said through trembling lips. "My mouth Sir, is hungry for your boots. Sir, if you see fit to allow me to just kiss them once I will be grateful."

I smiled down at him and raised one of my booted feet to his mouth. He kissed the tip of my boot and I put my foot quickly down on the floor. I could tell from the way he kept his tongue hanging out of his mouth that he was hoping for another kiss at my boot. Well, he could hope all he wanted to. A little anticipation is good for a boy who is in training.

"Thank you Sir," Bobby whispered down at my feet.

"You'll stay kneeling there for as long as I say," I said to him. "You got a problem with that Bobby?"

"No Sir, no problem at all Sir," he replied with the utmost respect.

"I'm going to do things to you that you will not believe Bobby," I said sternly. "I'm going to put you through hell and you're going to thank me for all of it."

Not looking up at me Bobby simply nodded. I could see his exquisite lips pouting and the tears that he was choking back flooding his eyes. As Bobby knelt next to me with his head hanging down I reached into my pants pocket and brought out a long black bandanna. He didn't flinch as I tied it over his eyes, blindfolding him. Actually, he didn't resist at all as I blindfolded him. I decided to test the waters a tad more. I picked up his beer bottle and sniffed the rim of it. The scent of Bobby's saliva on the bottle sent chills through me. I licked the rim of his bottle and savored the taste of his saliva in my mouth. I looked at him and silently mouthed the words, "I love you." I put the bottle to his lips and fed him what was left of the beer.

"Th-thank you Sir," Bobby said softly when he was done drinking.

I slid the neck of the bottle into his sweet mouth and forced him to suck it like it was a cock. Again he didn't resist, he simply took it. With my hand on the back of his neck he sucked that bottle neck like crazy. When I took the bottle out of his mouth his tongue hung beautifully and pleadingly out of his mouth. I knew he wanted more than just a bottle to suck on. I placed two of my fingers to his mouth and he instantly slurped at them. Chills coursed through me like mad as the kid suckled the fuck out of my fingers, so lovingly; sucking them like they were two cocks I was feeding him. He had the suction of a vacuum cleaner, ha! Needless to say my cock was rage hard and pounding in my leather pants. After a while I pulled my fingers slowly from Bobby's mouth, pressed the tips of them against his trembling lips and told him to relax, indicating that that was enough, for the moment.

"Want another cold beer now?" I asked him.

"Sir, only if you say so," Bobby replied with respect in his voice.

"Good boy, that's what I want to hear," I said proudly.

I looked down at Steve as he tended bar. When he saw me looking down at him I held up two fingers. He nodded. I watched as Steve told one of the busboy's to temporarily tend the bar for him. Then, with two fresh cold beers Steve ascended the stairs and came over to my table. At the sight of Bobby kneeling before me with his head hanging down and blindfolded Steve smiled from ear to ear.

"Glad to see that you two have hit it off pretty well," Steve said.

Bobby licked his lips nervously at the sound of Steve's voice. As Steve placed the beers on the table and twisted the tops off them I placed a reassuring hand on the back of Bobby's neck.

"Enjoy," Steve said and walked off.

Other couples had settled at tables close by where Bobby and I were. I noticed that another master had followed my example. He had his boy kneeling beside him as well, although his boy wasn't blindfolded. I picked up one of the fresh beers and put the tip of the bottle to Bobby's quivering lips.

"Drink up boy," I said, one hand holding the bottle to his mouth, the other on the back of his neck.

Bobby sipped the beer as I gently caressed the back of his beautiful neck...

A short while later the beer was halfway done and Bobby was again seated across from me. I had taken the blindfold off him. I wanted to train him slowly, not bombard him with everything at once. And God knew that if he did decide to be *my* boy he would have lots of training to endure. God there was so much I planned to put this beautiful fucking guy through.

"So Bobby, what are your living arrangements at the present time?" I asked him and sipped my fresh beer.

"I live alone Sir," Bobby replied. "Which is why I'm glad that my job pays so well. You see Sir, I live here in Manhattan."

"Good for you," I said, sounding impressed. "You must have moved out of your parent's house when you were very young."

"Actually Sir, I lived with my uncle from the time I was ten years old," Bobby said and his lips suddenly pursed tightly together after having said it. "You see Sir, my parents, they uh, my parents died in a car accident when I was ten. My uh, my uncle Charlie took me in and became my legal guardian. He was, is, my only real relative. He's my father's younger brother. I lived with him until a year or so ago when I started making good money at my job. I felt that he had done enough for me and I didn't want to be a burden to him. He said that I wasn't a burden but he didn't exactly stand in my way of leaving."

Bobby leaned back in his chair and folded his arms tightly in front of him, holding his lips pursed tightly together.

"Oh God Bobby," I said softly.

"I'm over it man, sorry, SIR! I'm over it Sir!" Bobby said, holding up a hand. "Please Sir, I, I don't want you feeling sorry for me. I know; I know that my parents loved me and it was just a freak accident that took them from me."

He grabbed his beer, said he was sorry for calling me "man" instead of Sir and took a long swig of his brew. I saw that the kid was choking on his tears. I moved my chair around close to his and gathered him into my arms. He put his arms around me and clung to me fiercely. I kissed the back of his neck, inhaling his rugged yet vulnerable scent. He shook in my arms and I whispered that it was okay. It was okay for him to let his emotions show. As he shook harder I held him and he let it go for a few moments. When we stopped hugging Bobby looked into my eyes with fierce determination.

"Sir, train me, train me Sir to be your slave," he said urgently. "I will gladly take anything you dish out on me. My only wish is to please you Master Kent, *please Sir.*"

I stood up, pointed at the floor and he instantly knelt in front of me, his hands resting on the sides of my boots. He leaned down further and kissed the tips of my boots.

"Anything Bobby?" I asked him, the gruffness having returned to my voice. "You'll take anything that I dish out on you?"

"Anything Sir," he replied, looking down at my boots. "I feel like my life has changed tonight, totally. And in such a short time at that Sir."

"Then the training *will* begin here, tonight," I said, taking the black blindfold from my pants pocket again. "On your feet boy!"

When I descended the stairs a while later Bobby was beside me, blindfolded, his hands cuffed behind him and a plain leather collar around his neck. His tee shirt was off him and hanging out of my back pocket like a big handkerchief. His muscular chest was bared for all to see. He was proportioned beautifully, his body sculpted in muscle. I held his arm tightly, leading him over to the bar.

"Another beer boy?" I asked him.

"Sir, only if you're having one," Bobby replied dutifully.

I stood at the end of the bar with him beside me. His work buddies were still there and looking at us as if dumbstruck. They could not believe the sight of their work supervisor now. Actually, I think they were feeling jealous as well as awed. Steve came over to me.

"Like I said, it sure looks like you two hit it off rather well," Steve said, taking in the sight of Bobby and me.

"Y-yes we did," Bobby said, obviously recognizing Steve's voice from earlier.

"Boy, you will speak only when I grant you permission to do so," I seethed softly in Bobby's ear, holding his upper arm in a tight and burning grasp. *"Is that clear?"*

"Y-yes Sir," Bobby replied quickly, grimacing behind the blindfold.

"Two beers Master Kent?" Steve asked me with respect.

"Make it just one Steve," I said sternly, looking at Bobby.

I was sure that he was able to feel my steely glare boring into him.

"One beer for me," I said to Steve. "I'll give my boy here a nice warm drink after I'm done. After chugging a few beers I always have to piss like a racehorse."

Bobby's lips pouted at the prospect of drinking my piss, but he didn't complain at all. Already he was devoted to me. I would teach him the joys of scoffing down his master's piss. Before we had descended the stairs I had told Bobby that he could avoid this entire humiliating experience of being paraded around in bondage simply by saying the safe word that I had chosen. The word was blue. I had chosen the word blue because, as I told my boy, that's how his balls would always feel, blue. He would always have a raging case of blue balls as he would not be permitted to shoot his load very often. He replied by telling me that he wanted to please me, and if pleasing me meant parading him around my bar shirtless handcuffed and blindfolded then he would do it. Steve handed me a fresh cold beer and I took a long swig of it. Bobby's work buddies were still staring at us in amazement.

"Your buddies are staring," I said to Bobby. "Would you care to tell them that you won't be accompanying them for the ride home?"

"Yes Sir, if you say so Sir," Bobby said huskily.

I guided him over to where his buddies were still seated at the bar.

"Hey guys," Bobby called out as if his friends were far off in the distance.

"We're here Bobby," the guy who had been sitting next to Bobby earlier said and reached out to touch my boy.

I quickly yanked Bobby back, closer to me. I looked at the guy with fire in my eyes.

"G-guys, I'll be spending the night with Master Kent," Bobby said in a husky tone of voice. "Actually, he's invited me for the weekend. As you can see I've been collared."

I took a gulp of my beer, as Bobby's buddies seemed to consider what he had just said.

"Are you sure this is what you want man?" one of the guys who were standing asked Bobby.

"You know it Ron," Bobby said through trembling lips. "You know it more than anybody man. Remember the conversations we've had?"

The guy named Ron stepped close to Bobby and squeezed his arm, the one I wasn't holding.

"Good luck Robert," Ron said happily and then looked at me sternly and winked. "Be good to him Master Kent. He's a special boy."

I simply took a long gulp of my beer, tightened my grip on Bobby's arm and walked away from the bar with him. I saw patrons of the bar looking at Bobby with hunger in their eyes. When Master Jeff saw me with my new slave boy his eyes lit up like two shining stars. I walked Bobby over to where he and his boy Chris were participating in a game of Pool.

"Well, and what do we have here?" Master Jeff asked me. "Looks like my suggestion paid off eh Kent?"

I told Master Jeff that fate seemed to have shined on me that night. He looked at Bobby hungrily and lustfully.

"Master Jeff, this is my boy Bobby, Boy, this is my good buddy, Master Jeff," I said, making the introductions. "Say hello Boy."

"G-good to meet you Master Jeff," Bobby said politely and I quickly noted how he did not call Master Jeff "Sir."

The word "Sir" would be reserved only for me in Bobby's vocabulary, good boy.

"It's good to meet you too Boy," Master Jeff responded and squeezed one of Bobby's pointy nipples, jiggling it hard.

Bobby grimaced behind his blindfold and moved closer to me. I think he felt confused when I didn't make Master Jeff let go of his nipple. Jeff's slave boy Chris sidled over to us and gave Bobby's other nipple a tight hard squeeze. Again my boy grimaced...

"Good looking piece of beef you got here Master Kent," Chris said mockingly. "You plan to train him?"

"I'm training him now," I said gruffly to the sarcastic slave boy.

Master Jeff and I didn't introduce Bobby and Chris to each other. There was no need to. They were slaves after all. That was all they needed to know about each other. What I could not believe was how Master Jeff's slave had spoken to me without permission from his master. I wondered if my buddy would dole out punishment for that upon his boy. Holding Bobby's arm in a firm and reassuring grip I allowed Master Kent and slave boy Chris to tweak and squeeze my boy's nipples. Bobby soon realized that by allowing my friend and his slave to tease his nipples he was pleasing and trusting me. He knew that as long as I was there that I wouldn't allow any harm to come to him. Master Jeff's Pool playing friend gestured over to him and Chris. Master Jeff said that it looked like he and Chris were up. They let go of Bobby's nipples and my boy breathed a sigh of ecstatic relief.

"Enjoy the rest of the night," I said to the two men as they walked back to the pool table.

"You too Kent, train that boy right," Master Jeff replied meanly.

"I intend to," I said brashly, making sure Bobby understood.

He did. The bar was getting even more crowded. The mass of bodies was causing the place to get warmer as well. The scent of man sweat mixed with leather was becoming overpowering. Bobby was starting to sweat profusely yet he didn't complain. With my hand that was holding the cold beer bottle I ran a fingertip gingerly over his sweat covered chest, tweaked one of his nipples good and hard and took a long scoff down of my beer.

"Feeling good boy?" I asked him sternly.

"Yes Sir," Bobby responded respectfully.

I smiled with satisfaction. The need to piss had set in but I wanted to wait till I was done with my beer, then I would really test my boy's allegiance to me...

A short while later I was done with my beer. My cock was piss hard in my leather pants. Holding the empty bottle in hand I led my blindfolded boy toward the men's room, holding him now by the D-ring in the leather collar around his neck. In the dimly lit bathroom the scents of piss, sweat and whiskey filled the air. Even though he couldn't see Bobby did not need three guesses to know where he was now. The bathroom has three stalls, two urinals and two sinks. I chuckled meanly because I was about to make my boy into a third urinal. Two of the stalls were being used one with a guy pissing in it and the other inhabited by two guys, one sucking the other's cock. Only one of the urinals was being used, the other one was vacant.

"Okay boy, over this way," I said meanly, guiding Bobby over to the vacant urinal against the wall. "Now, knees!"

Without a word Bobby slid to his knees in front of me.

"Head back boy," I said sternly.

"Y-yes Sir," Bobby said softly and leaned his head back against the urinal he was kneeling in front of.

The guy at the urinal next to the one I had Bobby kneeling in front of finished his pissing, zipped up and walked off. I took my big cock out of my leather pants and gently placed the tip of it against my boy's lips. He sniffed it a few times and then stuck out his tongue, lapped at the slit of my big meat and sniffed it some more. His face showed awe behind his blindfold as he took a deep breath. It was obvious how much the kid wanted my huge manhood.

"OHHHHH GOD Sir," Bobby panted. "Pl-please, the blindfold."

"It stays on boy, until I say otherwise," I replied sternly and slapped my semi hard cock against his cheek. "Now, down the hatch."

Bobby dutifully opened his mouth and I positioned my slit over it. I pissed in spurts into his mouth, wanting him to be able to swallow it all.

"Ohhhhhh, that feels a lot better, what a relief," I grunted as I pissed a hot rancid yellow stream into the kid's eager mouth. "Every morning you'll do this for me boy."

"Y-yes Sir," Bobby said softly after swallowing the piss I had just fed him, his mouth hung open instantly for more.

I placed the tip of my now hard cock between his lips and pissed hard into his mouth. The kid chugged it down greedily, running the tip of his tongue lovingly over the crown of my hardness.

"OHHHHHHH GAWD feels so fucking good," I rasped.

A couple of the guys who were now in the men's room watched as my newfound boy dutifully chugged down my hot steaming piss.

"Looks like a real hot boy you got there Master Kent," a buddy of mine said, stepping to my side as I finished pissing.

"Yeah, that is for sure," I replied and a shiver sped through me as the guy leaned down, pulled my leather vest aside and respectfully kissed one of my big nipples, rubbing the bottom of my hugely muscled pec as he did so.

The guy walked off and I slowly slid my hard cock out of Bobby's mouth. He licked his lips thoroughly drinking down my piss that had accumulated there. I was aching to fuck the kid's mouth and make him swallow my load next, but there was time for that. There was time for that and so much more. Bobby knelt there in front of me with his tongue hanging out as I packed my huge cock back into my pants and zipped up.

"Need to piss boy?" I asked him, placing my fingers under his chin.

"O-only with your permission Sir," Bobby replied.

"On your feet boy," I ordered and Bobby pulled himself to his feet and stood practically at attention in front of me.

I looked him over and my heart swelled with the utmost pride.

"You're making me real proud boy," I said and quickly kissed his cheek.

"Th-thank you Sir, I hope that I can continue to make you just as proud," Bobby responded.

Then, I turned him around facing the urinal and pulled the zipper down on his jeans. He inhaled deeply as I reached in past his sweaty underpants. With my other arm draped over his upper body I brought Bobby's big meat stick out of his pants. He was hard as concrete, painfully hard it almost seemed. Chuckling, I pulled more and brought out his beautiful and sexy nut sac. His balls hung down beautifully in his sac, obviously filled with torrents of his construction worker boy juices. Bobby was breathless as I held his cock over the urinal, my strong arm draped over him, my lips pressed against the back of his beautiful neck.

"Ohhhhh God Sir," Bobby gasped joyously as I handled him, making a huge production over allowing him to piss.

"Piss now boy," I commanded and Bobby said "Yes Sir."

He took a deep breath and did just as I told him to do, he pissed long and hard and frothy into the urinal. If he looked ecstatic while he was pissing I wondered just how he would look when he shot his load. But, there was time for that. If Bobby decided to be my boy one of the first things he would have to learn would be that he could only shoot his load when I told him he could. And that would not be all that often. I wanted my boy always horny, always on the edge, always ready and in the mood to serve me. Bobby pissed a good long hot steaming mess of yellow piss into the urinal as I held him close to me.

"Good boy," I said when he was done.

He gasped feverishly as I slid his semi hard cock roughly back into his jeans along with those big juicy sweat soaked testicles of his. I zipped him up and turned him back around facing me. Without being told to he kissed me on the cheek.

"Thank you Sir," Bobby whispered and I pulled him close to me, hugging him intensely.

I could feel his heart pounding against my chest. I kissed the side of his neck and reached down and grabbed a handful of one of his bubble butt cheeks. I squeezed his ass hard…

A few moments later I exited the bathroom with Bobby, holding his arm tight as we walked back out to the bar. As we approached the shoeshine stand I told Bobby that my boots needed shining.

"Yes Sir," he said dutifully.

Within a few moments I was seated on the shoeshine chair and Bobby was standing there at my feet, running and slathering his tongue over my propped up feet in their boots. He didn't protest once as Master Jeff and his slave boy Chris stood at his sides, teasing and tweaking his nipples. My handcuffed and blindfolded boy simply did as I had told him and polished up my boots with his tongue.

"Great looking kid you got here Kent," Master Jeff said and squeezed one of Bobby's nipples real hard.

Bobby grimaced in pain, took a deep breath and continued sliding his tongue over my boots.

"Yeah, real fucking great looking," slave boy Chris said tweaking the fuck out of Bobby's other nipple. "Looking at him makes me want to test my dominant side and work him over for a while. What do you say Master Kent, how about giving Master Jeff and I some time with this guy of yours?"

Bobby stopped tonguing my boots for a split second and looked up at me in blindfolded horror.

"When pigs fly out of my butt you vulture," I said meanly to Chris and watched as my boy went back to shining up my boots with his tongue, a look of relief now on his face.

"You know Bobby, my master here made me drink your piss out of the urinal you pissed in before," Chris said snidely to Bobby, his fingers tweaking and teasing his nipple. "You taste like magic is all I can say. Amazing that a guy's piss could taste so good huh? But then, being as hot looking as you are I wasn't all that surprised. How does it feel knowing that your piss is now inside me?"

Bobby paid no mind to Master Jeff and Chris as they went on teasing and tweaking his nipples. He simply ran his tongue up the side of one of my boots, flicking his tongue over it as he went. As far as he was concerned the two men teasing him weren't even there.

"He loves you Bobby, I can see it," Chris whispered in Bobby's ear, glancing up at me as he did so. "Everyone will love you…"

After a while Master Jeff and his slave Chris wandered off and Bobby finished his work on my boots.

"Seems like those two so called friends of mine really have the eye for you," I said to Bobby, standing next to him, holding his arm in a tight grip again.

"Yes Sir, they really seem to," Bobby said. "But they don't mean anything to me."

Bobby leaned in close to me and I put an arm around him, hugged him tight and kissed the top of his head.

"You ready to head over to my place for the night boy?" I asked him.

"Yes Sir, if you're ready then so am I," Bobby said.

"You won't be getting all that much sleep boy," I said meanly. "As a matter of fact you won't be getting any sleep until I say so. Is that clear?"

Bobby gulped hard and said, "Yes Sir."

With a sadistic looking smile on my face I walked Bobby out of the bar and to my car that was parked across the street from the place. I settled the kid into the passenger seat and lowered his blindfold. Sitting in the driver's seat I cupped his chin in my hand and turned him facing me.

"Good God almighty, but you truly are the most glorious looking young man I have ever seen Bobby," I said and gently kissed his lips.

"Now remember, like in the bar you can avoid all that is going to happen to you tonight simply by saying the word blue."

Bobby nodded his head "no" and instead said, "Sir, take me home, take me home Master Kent and train me." I forced his mouth open and spit heartily twice into it. The kid grimaced and dutifully swallowed my saliva. Then, I released his chin and started the car...

We arrived at my house a little later.

"I own this three bedroom house," I said to Bobby as I parked the car in the driveway. "The third bedroom and the basement are both fashioned as dungeons of sorts. The third bedroom is where you will be spending most of your time tonight and tomorrow as well. You're in for a shit load of torture boy. I'm going to work you like never before in your life."

"Nice looking house Sir," Bobby said, looking at me in the dimly lit driveway.

With the motor still running in the car I grabbed a handful of Bobby's hair and pulled him toward me.

"What did I tell you back in the bar boy?" I asked him, my face right in his, my lips grazing his.

"Owwwwwww, Sir, y-you told me not to speak unless you gave me permission Sir," Bobby said through trembling lips. "I-I'm sorry Sir, I won't fuck up again!"

"Damn right you won't boy!" I said meanly and forced his mouth open.

I again spit into his mouth, three good ones this time. Bobby gulped down my saliva and I let go of his hair. He slumped back in the seat, gasping and catching his breath. Looking at him sitting there in the passenger seat of my car, shirtless with his hands cuffed behind him looking totally petrified my breath caught in my throat. I shut off the car after getting it parked and leaned in close to the kid, hooking an arm around him.

"Damn it boy, what am I going to do about all this?" I asked him in a husky tone of voice.

Bobby looked at me with those puppy dog eyes of his and I kissed him hard on the mouth. Before getting out of the car I took the handcuffs off him and gave him back his tee shirt, temporarily.

With his shirt in hand Bobby climbed out of the car and quickly dashed around to my side to open my door for me.

"Get that shirt on boy," I said to him as we walked toward the front of my house.

Without a word Bobby did as he was told.

Once in the house I brought the boy directly to the third bedroom, the dungeon...

Within in a few minutes the kid was stripped to his white sweat socks which were tucked down around his ankles and his sweaty piss stained white briefs. I had him stretched out and lashed at the wrists and ankles to the rack that dominated the epicenter of the room. His huge hard cock and juicy balls were sticking out of the fly opening of his briefs. I didn't want his cock rubbing against anything, thus preventing him from shooting his load if he thought to. I built the rack myself I'm proud to say. It stands in a diagonal position in the very center of the room. I cannot tell you just how magnificent and how sexy Bobby looked as he squirmed around in erotic helplessness on the device. Actually, my beautiful newfound boy didn't have one single iota of the misery he was about to endure on the rack. My cock pounded with the years of pent-up need for this moment. And it seemed that fate had wanted me to wait especially for Bobby. As he lay there stretched out and tightly bound I gathered a few more things from around the dungeon/room that I would need. Bobby wasn't blindfolded but he simply stared straight ahead as I did what I had to do, not uttering a word, only grunting and panting. Droplets upon droplets of pre cum oozed from the kid's wide sexy slit and slithered down the eight to nine inch shaft of his meat pole. Fuck, he loved all of this already. He was a true slave boy if ever there was one and I had to thank the gods for bringing him to me. I silently prayed to the one true God to grant me this beautiful boy for the rest of my life. Bobby's muscular body writhed beautifully in the bondage. His hairy armpits were stinking and dripping with man sweat. What a fucking awesome sight he was. When I was done gathering the devices I would need I stepped over to the rack and put the stuff down on a small table next to the structure.

"Feeling good boy?" I asked him and meanly jiggled one of his very fleshy and very pointy nipples.

He simply looked at me and did not utter a word. I smiled meanly but proudly.

"You've got permission to speak boy," I said to him and gave his nipple a squeeze.

"Y-yes Master Kent, Sir, if it makes you feel good to do this to me, th-then I feel really good," Bobby responded.

"Well, you won't be feeling all that good pretty soon boy," I said, placing my hand on a wheel hooked up to the restraints on Bobby's stretched out ankles and wrists. "Now, brace yourself."

The kid clenched his teeth and I gave the wheel a turn, causing the restraints to stretch him out even further and even more painfully.

"YAAAARHHHHHHH OHHHH GOD!!" he screamed in agony and I turned the wheel a second time. "AAAYYYRRRRR!!!"

Bobby's handsome face congealed into a look of out-rights pain and agony. Tears filled his eyes. He clenched his hands into fists and braced himself for the third turn of the wheel. He screamed like a man in pain as I turned the wheel a third time. Now he was really stretched good and fucking taut. No doubt his head was spinning as he suffered erotically. His cock though remained rigidly hard all throughout the torture. I took my hands off the wheel, stepped close to his handsome face and cupped his chin in my hand. He looked at me in agony through his beautiful tear soaked eyes.

"Say the word blue and I'll stop boy," I said to him. "Permission to speak granted…"

"N-no Sir, *I-I want to make you proud of me Master Kent,*" he squeaked and I leaned down and kissed him on the mouth.

His lips trembled against mine as I kissed him, reached for one of his nipples and gave it a nasty squeeze. When I stopped kissing him I stepped to the foot of the table, squatted between Bobby's bound socked ankles and took hold of the wheel that was at that end of the table, hooked up only to the restraints on his feet. I began turning the wheel which caused Bobby's separately bound feet to spread apart, exposing a part of him that I wanted access to, his gaping pink and tight rosebud of an asshole.

"UHHHHHNNNNN," he panted as his legs were pulled wide apart.

"Ingenious device this rack, wouldn't you say boy?" I asked him.

"Y-yes Sir Master Kent," Bobby gurgled.

When his legs were spread good and fucking wide I stood up and stepped next to his face again.

"You thirsty boy?" I asked him.

Bobby looked at me miserably and nodded "Yes", that he was thirsty. From the table where I had put the devices of erotic torture I planned to use on the kid I picked up a bottle of cold mineral water. I opened it and put it to Bobby's lips. He held his head up and gulped it down gratefully.

"Heh, heh, bet you thought I was going to make you drink piss again eh boy?" I asked him.

He drank more than half the bottle of water and I kissed his lips again. Then, from the table next to the rack I picked up a long fat dildo shaped plastic vibrator.

"You ready for some real fun Bobby?" I asked him, holding up the device in plain view.

"If, if you say so Sir," he replied, his splayed legs squirming back and forth.

He knew all too well where that device was going.

"Now that I've given you a hearty drink that sexy mouth of yours should be good and wet eh Bobby?" I asked him, holding the device to his lips. "Get this thing good and fucking wet Boy!"

I slowly slid the device into his mouth as far as he could take it. I didn't want to choke him with the thing after all. Amazingly, he took more of it into his mouth then I thought he could possibly handle. He drooled all over the thing and sucked it hard his tear soaked eyes looking up beseechingly into mine. I flicked the switch on the side of the thing and it buzzed to life. Bobby's eyes crossed for a second and I could see that a dizzy sensation had come over him as the thing vibrated gratingly in his beautiful mouth.

"And hold it there," I whispered to him and let go of the thing, leering meanly down at him. "Got to get that hole of yours visible and ready."

Watching me and sucking heartily on the buzzing device in his mouth as his head obviously spun Bobby seemed miserable as I moved to the space between his spread legs. I took a pair of sharp tweezers from the table where I had placed the devices I had collected and then squatted between his beautiful muscular legs. I ran a hand over one of his calves, snapped the elastic in one of his socks against his skin and pressed the tip of my nose against his underpants, right where his hole was underneath, his hole, his hole that would be mine and mine only, *forever.* I sniffed the kid's shit chute through his underpants and his scent was raw and funky, vulnerable somehow. His big balls hung down in my face and I gave them a good slathering lick.

"God almighty Bobby, I love you my boy," I whispered, though I doubt he heard me.

As he sucked and sucked the vibrating dildo, getting it good and wet for the trip it was going to take into his hole I began snipping away the fabric of Bobby's underpants, slowly, slowly revealing his most private orifice. His legs squirmed and it made his hole breathe and stink even more. I gasped breathlessly as the boys most private of parts were revealed to me. I whispered again that I loved him, I truly adored him. When his hole was thoroughly exposed I put the tweezers down on the floor amid the tatters of his sheared underpants. Now he looked even sexier with his big manhood and balls sticking out of his torn up underpants and his hole exposed for me.

"Oh God," I grunted and spit liberally into his twitching, gaping and pink hole.

I watched as my saliva was literally sucked up by his ass lips and I spit twice more into it. The kid grunted and groaned breathlessly at that point as he suckled the buzzing device. I slowly slid two fingers into his hole.

"RRRRFFFF!!!" Bobby groaned loudly now, the buzzing making his poor head spin some more.

I twisted my fingers around in him, prodded his hole and drove him batty with the ecstasy. His hole was good and sopped with my saliva and stinking as well from the long day. When I pulled my fingers out of him I gave his hole a few licks and flicks with my tongue.

"Mmmm, nice tasting raunchy boy hole," I murmured.

"RRRRFFFF!!!" Bobby grunted and I glanced up to see a look of ecstasy mixed with misery on his angelic face.

"Yeah, you're ready boy," I said and got to my feet with a mean looking grin on my face.

Pre cum was oozing like crazy from Bobby's sexy cock slit. I stepped next to him and took the dildo out of his mouth. His lips were pouting and trembling. He was scared like never before in his life.

"Who's hole is that that I just moistened up with my saliva boy?" I asked him meanly, twisting one of his nipples a little more than hard.

"Y-your hole Sir, it's your hole," Bobby replied breathlessly, almost crying. "OHHHH GAWD Sir, *I'm in such pain.*"

"Want to say the safe word boy?" I asked him, moving back to between his legs, not able to wait to see his hole, my hole, again.

"N-no Sir, no, I-I'll make you proud Master Kent, always!!" Bobby panted and squirmed his pained stretched out torso on top of the rack. "OHHRRRRR!!!"

Always. He said it. But would he mean it? Always! Was he only saying it from the pain he was in? Always! I choked on my tears of joy and slid to my knees between his legs, the dildo in my hand.

"Good boy," I said. "Now relax and you'll do well throughout this."

I pressed the tip of the vibrating dildo against the walls and front of Bobby's hole.

"UUUHHNNNNN, GOD," the kid seethed in a mixture of torment and ecstasy as the buzzing dildo drove him crazy as it entered him.

I slid it in slowly, a little at a time. I wanted to see just how much he could actually take. At the first sign that he was truly suffering and not enjoying it at the same time I would stop. Unlike those monsters Cleeve and Otis I wanted to train my boy, not hurt him unnecessarily. But Bobby was the slave boy that I had hoped and prayed for. He was able to take the entire dildo into his hole. Actually, his hole seemed to be sucking the thing in, begging for it. The scent of the walls of his hole wafted up at me and my cock grew harder and harder in my leather pants. I could not wait till it was my boner in there fucking this beautiful, beautiful guy. When the dildo was all the way in I pulled it halfway out and slid it back in again, repeating this more than a few times, fucking the tar out of my newfound slave's hole.

"AAAARRRRHHHH, ohhhhhhh yeah, Oh Master Kent Sir, AAAAHHHHH!!!" Bobby grunted and groaned atop the rack.

"Okay boy, squeeze your ass hole good and tight around this thing," I instructed him. "I want to keep it in there while I work you over somewhere else on that succulent body of yours."

"Y-yes Master Kent, yes Sir!" Bobby replied and did as I said. "OOOHHRRRRR fuuuucccckkkk, goddamned thing is making me crazy, sounds and feels like a million bees are buzzing in my asshole!!!"

I got to my feet and saw that Bobby's cock was rigidly hard, his balls big and bulging, no doubt storing up a load big enough to choke a horse. Massive droplets of pre cum now oozed from his slit and slid down the sides of his shaft.

"Feeling good boy?" I asked him and leaned down to lick some of the pre cum off the side of his cock.

Chris had been right earlier. Bobby tasted like magic. More than anything at that moment I wanted to make him cum and cum and cum, but he had to wait, *he had to earn it.*

"Y-yes Master Kent, I-I feel like I'm flying Sir," Bobby panted, sweating and squirming on the rack, heaving.

"Heh, then lets bring you in for a landing boy," I said meanly and placed my hands on the wheel on the rack, giving it a half twist, stretching my boy some more.

"AAAYYRRRR!!!" Bobby screamed in pain and I saw that the dildo slid somewhat out of him.

"Squeeze that hole tight boy," I ranted down at him. "If that dildo falls out of you it's twenty lashes!"

"Y-yes Sir!!" Bobby blubbered, tears streaming down his face, the desire to please me overwhelming him.

He squeezed his ass lips tightly together and I swear his hole sucked that thing right back in. Smiling down at him I gave his chest a rub and his nipples a fast squeeze each.

"You're magnificent Bobby," I whispered and leaned down to kiss him on the mouth. "No one, not even Master Jeff and his vulture of a slave boy Chris will ever touch you again, I promise that."

"Th-thank you Master Kent, an-anything you say Sir," Bobby replied.

I picked up a pair of tit clamps and held them up for him to see. They were the non-sharp teethed style. This would be the last bit of torture for that night. I couldn't keep him on that rack much longer anyway, he was starting to suffer a bit too much and that's not what I wanted. He looked like a sacrificial victim at some bizarre ritual the way I had that boy stretched out and tethered to the rack. As I have stated I wanted to train my boy, not severely hurt him. (It makes me crazy with rage when I think of how Cleeve and Otis hurt my boy.) At the sight of the tit clamps Bobby's eyes opened wide with a mixture of fear and anticipation. I leaned down again and this time slurped one of his meaty nipples into my mouth. I know how to get my boy's nuts really churning, get one of his nipples up and erect, clamp it and then work the other one before clamping it. I love the fact that my boy has such sensitive nipples. He reeled and moaned in anguish atop the rack as I bit, nipped and sucked at his pink nub. The tip of it grew harder than hard against the tip of my tongue. I was aching at that point to shoot my load into my boy, my beautiful, beautiful boy…

When Bobby's first nipple was totally erect I clipped one of the tit clamps onto it, good and fucking tight.

"AAARRHHHHHH!!!" he screamed like a real man in pain.

His cock sloughed more pre cum and I quickly slurped his other nipple into my mouth, neither of us uttering a word, just accepting our roles in this fantasy/reality being played out. Bobby's other nipple reacted and came to life and hardness as fast as the first one had. When it was ready I clipped the second tit clamp onto it, sending more searing and erotic pain through him.

"AAAYYYRRRRRR!!! GOD, oh Master Kent, *pl-please Sir,*" Bobby whimpered, lifting his head up off the table and looking down at his suffering and sweat soaked muscular body.

"Tell me Bobby, tell me what you want boy," I said to him consolingly, stroking his forehead. "God, you *are truly the most beautiful young man I have ever known.*"

I leaned down and gently kissed his trembling lips.

"Tell me what you want boy," I said, my lips over his, grazing them, tasting his saliva and overwhelmed by his beauty.

"I-I want to cum Master Kent Sir, *I need to shoot my load, OHHHHRRR GOD please,*" he pleaded desperately.

I smiled down at him and the only sound we heard was the buzzing of the dildo embedded deep in my boy's hole.

"Bobby, part of your training here tonight, besides the pain and ecstasy you are experiencing is to know that you are to shoot your load only with my permission," I said to him softly but sternly.

"Oh God, please, *Master Kent Sir, I'll do anything,*" Bobby whimpered.

"I know you will Bobby," I said reassuringly and pulled slightly on the chain attached to the tit clamps. "And learning to shoot your load only when I say you can is the main thing you will do for me. *Is that understood boy?*"

A look of dismay mixed with uncertainty filled his beautiful eyes for a moment, but then through his trembling lips he said, "Y-yes Master Kent Sir, whatever you say Sir!"

"I'll teach you boy and you'll do well," I said to him. "I will make sure you do well. For the times where you do not do well I will paddle your ass and whip you, but even those things you will learn are for your benefit."

"Y-yes Master Kent, yes Sir!!" Bobby seethed on the rack.

"Good boy," I said with pride and stepped between his legs.

Slowly, so slowly I pulled the dildo from his saliva and sweat sopped hole.

"OHHHHRRRR fuck," Bobby railed when the dildo was out. "OHHHRRRR GAWD, my hole, oh fuck, what are you doing to me Master Kent???"

"Teaching you to control that load boy," I replied. "After having your hole filled and not shooting your load is enough to drive you crazy."

Grinning, I placed the dildo on the small table and then Bobby watched as I lowered the zipper on my leather pants. He gasped and panted at the sight of my huge sausage sized fat cock. Without a word I undid the restraints on his socked ankles, lifted his legs high, climbed aboard the rack between his legs and entered his exquisite and more than ready hole.

"OHHHHHRRR GODS," Bobby grunted as I slid halfway inside him.

His hole felt like velvet as I entered him inch by inch, sheer joy and ecstasy inside that boy of mine.

His hard cock pounded like crazy, twitched between his legs and oozed more and more pre cum.

"Please Master Kent, fuck me, *please fuck me hard Sir, make me your slave,"* Bobby pleaded.

"You are my slave Bobby, from this moment and until the end of time," I whispered and slid the rest of the way into him.

He screamed in animal abandon as I filled him and began thrusting in and out of him like crazy, his hole accommodating the entire length and girth of my huge man-meat. His hole was moist and tight. I cannot describe for you just how excellent it felt being inside him. As I fucked him Bobby cried tears of joy and pain, the rack and the tit clamps driving him nearly over the edge.

"Oh yeah, I'll release you as soon as I've filled this hole Bobby, your hole that's my hole now," I said with total authority.

"Y-yes Master Kent, yes," Bobby panted, his shackled hands clenched tightly into fists.

I held onto his calves, pumped in and out of his hole like crazy and then felt myself getting close.

"OH yeah, yeah, my beautiful fucking boy!!" I roared as I shot my giant load inside him. "OHHHHRRRRR FUUUCCCKKK!!!!"

"All the years of loneliness and waiting for a slave boy like Bobby came together and to an end in that moment of sheer and total joy, total joy as I filled Bobby's hole with my juices of love. With his head still raised he watched the expressions of ecstasy etched on my face as I seemed to cum and cum and cum inside him.

"Yes, shoot your load Master Kent, make me your slave boy," Bobby begged again.

"AAARRRHHHHHH!!!" I roared when the last glob of my *cum* spewed from me and drained into Bobby. "*I love you Bobby, I love you now and I will love you for more than a thousand years, I will love you for eternity that I promise you.*"

Slowly, my cock slid out of his hole and I quickly released him from the rack and removed his tit clamps. Sitting there on the rack he put his arms around me and we held each other close and tight. Bobby clung to me as if he would never let go…and he never has.

"I know you want to shoot that load of yours boy, but wait, I promise you'll love me for making you wait," I whispered in his ear, kissing his earlobe at the same time. "I love you boy."

"Yes Master Kent, anything for you, I love you too Sir," Bobby grunted, tears streaming down his face.

"Lets go to bed Bobby," I said and helped him off the rack.

I had him stretch his arms and legs, as if he had just worked out hard at the gym. After what I had just done to his arms and legs on the rack it was imperative that he stretch them out to keep the blood circulating properly. We walked to my master bedroom and fell asleep almost in minutes, our arms wrapped around each other. We slept that way the entire night.

Now, sitting there in our living room, holding the framed picture of Bobby it all came back to me in a flash, that wonderful night when we first met. Looking at his picture I whispered "I love you Bobby" over and over again…

That night at my leather bar…

Bobby came in after a long day at a construction site at about eight thirty. He looked tired and sweaty from slinging cinderblocks; hoisting two by fours and working with jackhammers and other tools. He walked over to the bar where Steve was working.

"Hey Bobby," Steve said as my boy walked over to him behind the bar. "How's it going?"

"Not too bad, just really winded from a long day in the hot sun," Bobby replied and the two men kissed each other on the cheek. "Can I bother you for a glass of club soda with some ice?"

"Sure thing bud, help yourself," Steve said as he served a customer in a big cowboy style hat a beer.

"Is Master Kent here?" Bobby asked as he filled a glass with ice and club soda.

"Yep," Steve replied and pointed to the second level of the bar where I was seated in my usual spot sipping a beer.

Bobby waved to me and I held up my hand, indicating that I had seen him.

"See you later Steve, thanks for the club soda," Bobby said and walked away from the bar, his glass in hand.

He sprinted up the steps toward me. Watching him dash up those steps made me remember again that first night we met. On that night he had come up the steps slowly and apprehensively, not knowing what to expect.

"Good evening Master Kent Sir," Bobby said and stood there before me.

God almighty, even after two years he would not sit down till I gave him permission to do so.

"Hi Bobby, sit down," I said to him, as always drinking in the sight of him in total awe.

"Any word on Officer McLaughlin?" Bobby asked as he sat down and sipped his club soda.

"Not a goddamned peep," I said dejectedly. "I'm beginning to wonder if they're ever going to let him go."

"*Shit!!*" Bobby said angrily. "Fucking bastards."

Sitting there we each sipped our drinks.

"You know, I heard that there was a real wild happening at "The Local" yesterday night," Bobby said. "Some of the more sleazy guys at the jobsite were jawing about it while we were having lunch."

"Really now?" I asked and grinned at my boy as we discussed the sleazy bar that was competition for mine. "And just what were those sleazy dudes jawing about boy?"

"Well Sir, they said that two burly guys came in there with the story that they were selling some cop's ass and charging them as well for him to give them head," Bobby said. "I thought it sounded like Cleeve and Otis had brought your cop buddy to "The Local" but then I thought how that was ridiculous, seeing as stuff like that goes on all the time at that bar."

"True Bobby, but then again, you never know..." I said. "Maybe we should run that past Officer Robinson when we talk to him again..."

"I tried calling you in the afternoon but you weren't home Sir," Bobby said to me.

"I was at headquarters with Officer Robinson," I said. "Hoping we would get some word."

"Well, let's hope we hear something soon," Bobby said and gulped down his club soda. "Ahhhhh man, I was thirsty."

"How was your day boy? Other than your sleazy co-workers talking about their escapades at "The Local" that is?" I asked my boy, still with that grin on my face whenever that sleazy establishment is part of the conversation.

As we talked I was holding his hand in mine. I could still feel his hand and fingers slightly trembling, they had been ever since his horrid experience with Cleeve and Otis. I wondered if I would have to suggest some therapy for my boy. Just like I had a good cop buddy I also had a good buddy who was a psycho-therapist. Doctor Andrew Carlson dealt a lot with trauma victims.

"Tiring Master Kent Sir, we worked all day in the hot sun," Bobby said.

"Let's head on home then," I suggested. "Did you have dinner?"

"Yeah, we ate at the site," Bobby said. "We had some Chinese food sent over..."

"Good deal, I had wanted to hang out here with you tonight, but I think you need your rest," I said to him.

"Thank you Master Kent Sir," Bobby said appreciateively.

We left the bar together and headed home in my car...

When we got to the house neither of us noticed the big blue van parked half a block away. My boy and I stepped out of the car and went in the house...

"Well, there they are Officer Stupid McLaughlin," Cleeve said, standing in the back of the van with my cop buddy, looking out a small window at Bobby and me. "Fuck man, but that boy of Master Kent's is succulent looking enough for another go round. And needless to say but Kent ain't so bad himself."

"RRRRMMMFFFFF!!!!" John seethed behind the duct tape that had been stuck tightly over his mouth.

The cop was standing propped against a back wall of the infamous van, the kidnap mobile if you would. His hands were cuffed behind him, locked again in his own handcuffs; his upper body was roped tight with mounds upon mounds of heavy duty rope wound around his muscular torso, pinning his well-muscled arms to his body. A short length of rope was tied around the poor captive cop's neck and the slack of it was tied off to a hook just a few inches above where he was standing. Even though his feet weren't tied any movement whatsoever would cause my good buddy to choke himself. His big Irish sized cock and swollen balls were hanging out of his uniform pants, said pants having been put back on him after those two monsters left "The Local" with him. His badge had been pinned to one of his poor exposed nipples, his uniform shirt, what remained of it hanging on his shoulders in tatters.

"Not to worry Officer Stupid, we don't usually go after the same mark twice," Cleeve said, turning and hooking a hand around John's upper arm. "Of course though, rules are always made to be broken."

"MMMMFFFFF!!!" John sputtered angrily at Cleeve as he stood there feeling the globs of sludge dripping from his overly fucked ass, staining his uniform pants.

His underpants were gone, seeing as Cleeve had auctioned them off just before they left "The Local" with him. It amazed my buddy that he was able to stand up at all, given the night he had endured previously.

"You make the call Officer," Cleeve said and gave John's nipple (the one without his badge clipped to it) a mean jiggle and squeeze. "Either you stay with us for another day or so or we go after that sweet boy Bobby again. Nod "yes" and we let you go and grab the kid, nod "no" and we leave him alone, *but you're ours for another day, maybe two.* And that means another night or two thrown in at "The Local" as well as spending some time at my house of horrors. And I'll tell you Cop, torturing the fuck out of you has been a pleasure like I cannot fucking describe to you."

John glanced down at the gun that was back in his holster around his waist, no way of getting to it though the way he was cuffed and strung up. He looked at Cleeve with eyes filled with anger, revulsion and helplessness. Spittle formed around the sides of the gagged cop's mouth. Cleeve took hold of the cop's cock and began stroking it, John nodded "No, no, no..."

"You care a lot for that kid I can tell," Cleeve said as John spewed his load all over the floor of the van, the feeling of Cleeve stroking him mixed with the pain in his rectum from the night before seeming to spur him on. "You're a decent man Officer Stupid."

"RRRRMMMFFF!!!" John squealed as he shot his cop-sized load.

"But not to worry, we didn't drive to the master and his boy's house just so we could lug your ass back to "The Local" all over again," Cleeve said and began undoing the rope around John's neck, a mean and maniacal look etched on his face. "But mark me well on this one Officer Stupid, we will be lugging *someone's* sexy ass back to my house tonight…"

John grimaced at the wad of cash that Cleeve waved in his face, all the money that had been made the night before at "The Local" when he'd had his ass and mouth relentlessly and totally fucked over. Cleeve then threw open the back doors of the van and holding John tight by his upper arm heaved him bodily out of the vehicle. My buddy hit the pavement hard…

"RRRMMMFFFFF!!!!" John sputtered angrily up at Cleeve.

Bobby and I were sitting in the living room, each of us sipping a cold beer when the doorbell rang.

"I'll get it Sir," Bobby said, standing up and walking to the door.

I heard the door open and then Bobby's voice calling frantically, "Master Kent, Master Kent!" over and over. I quickly ran to the door and there was my good buddy Officer McLaughlin. He was standing in the doorway, still handcuffed, gagged and he seemed to be in tremendous pain.

"Goddamn," I muttered angrily.

Bobby and I helped the poor cop into the house and quickly got him untied. Once his hands were freed of the cuffs (luckily the key was in his uniform pants pocket) he angrily pulled the duct tape off his mouth and took the rancid sweat sock that had been crammed in his craw out of his mouth.

"Fucking Otis, made me eat his goddamned sock sweat," John grunted.

"Fucking bastards!!" the cop went on and leaned back on the couch, packing his big cock and balls into his pants and zipping up.

"Hold still Officer McLaughlin," Bobby said, sitting down next to the cop and slowly and carefully taking his badge off his nipple.

"Easy Kid," John whimpered. "Fuck, but that hurts like all hell."

"Sorry,' Bobby said. "But we do have to get this thing off you."

"John, are you okay?" I asked him.

"Yeah, nothin' that won't heal in time, just my goddamned pride is really hurt, not to mention some real private parts of me," John replied.

Bobby had gotten the pin unhooked and he slowly slid it off John's nipple.

"OWWWWWWWWWW!!! Shit!!!!" the cop seethed. "Th-thanks Bobby."

Bobby then handed John his badge.

"Fucking bastards got away again," John ranted angrily. "They left me at your door and drove off right after Cleeve rang your bell."

"Shit, I told you Master Kent, we'll never get them, *never!*" Bobby said dejectedly.

"We'll get them Bobby, don't worry about that," John said and squeezed Bobby's shoulder. "Are you okay by the way?"

"I'm fine," Bobby said.

"Fucking psychos, captured me and brought me to "The Local", the cop said. "If I told you what happened to me there you would not believe it."

"Holy shit, a few of my buddies at work were talking about that today," Bobby said. "Somehow I had a feeling you were the cop they were mentioning..."

"Yeah, it was me Kid," John said and clipped his badge to his tattered uniform shirt. "Fucking totally humiliating the things those sleazy guys did to me let me tell you... Oh, before I forget, Cleeve squeezed this note into my pocket before they drove off."

John reached into his uniform pants pocket and brought out a thin piece of notepaper.

"They said it's for you Kent," the cop said and handed me the paper. "I'll let you read it but then I'll need it back for evidence purposes, just like the note they left when Bobby was returned. Fuck, got to file my own report on a cop's abduction, *mine!*"

"*Oh shit, holy fuck!!*" I said as I read the note.

"What is it Master Kent?" Bobby asked.

"Listen to this," I said and read the note out loud this time. "Dear Master Kent, sorry for the delay in returning your cop buddy Officer Stupid McLaughlin to you, but he sure was a treat to have around and he made us a good fistful of cash at your competition bar, "The Local.""

Please send our greetings to that succulent boy of yours; it will be a while before we forget him. He didn't look any the worse for wear when Otis saw him at your bar an hour or so ago as he served himself a club soda, while that cute bartender of yours, Steve, served Otis a beer."

Bobby's eyes opened wide in fear and sudden recognition.

"Oh shit, holy fuck is right Master Kent Sir, the guy in the cowboy hat," Bobby said. "*That was Otis!!*"

"What guy in the cowboy hat?" I asked Bobby, already knowing and fearing what he would say.

"He was sitting at Steve's bar when I got there earlier Sir," Bobby said to me and John. "He had the cowboy hat sort of pulled down to obscure his face. He didn't want me to see that it was him. Oh shit, *Steve!!*"

"We have to get to the bar Kent!!" John said, getting to his feet and cramming Otis' rancid sock into his uniform pants pocket.

"Are you sure you're okay to make it?" I asked him.

"More than sure, those fuckers tortured me and sold my ass to nearly every sleaze at "The Local" but they didn't break me, come on, that bartender is in a lot of danger," the cop said urgently.

The three of us headed for the door as John did his best to arrange his tattered uniform shirt on his torso.

"We'll have to use your car Kent," he said as we walked out of the house. "My cruiser is still among the missing so to speak."

"Sure thing," I replied.

We arrived at the bar a little while later and made our way through the crowd over to the bar where Steve had been tending earlier. I noticed how a few of the sleazier male patrons were taking in the sight of my cop buddy. I wondered if they were some of the sleazes he had mentioned earlier who'd had their way with him at "The Local." Steve's relief, a handsome young guy named Tyler was now at the bar.

"Tyler, where's Steve?" I barked at him as the three of us walked up to the bar.

Smiling Tyler said, "He told me that that hot looking cowboy he was serving had a van in the back of the parking lot. Said that the cowboy dude wanted to tip him right, if you know what I mean..."

"Oh no, oh shit," Bobby said and he, John and I looked at each other with total dismay and agony etched on our faces.

But then, we saw Steve heading back into the bar from the back entrance, still shirtless in all his muscular glory.

"Steve!" I called out as he came over to the three of us.

"Hey there Kent, Bobby," Steve said and looked at Officer McLaughlin lustfully, taking in the sight of his tattered uniform shirt. "Officer..."

"Are you alright Sir?" John asked the hunky bartender.

"Sure am, why?" Steve asked, looking a little perplexed, but still drinking in the sight of the handsome and rugged cop.

"Can I ask where you were just now?" my cop buddy asked him, sounding a little stern.

Steve looked at me with confusion written all over his face. I quickly told him that it was okay to answer the cop and that he wasn't in any trouble at all. Thank God he wasn't in any trouble.

"I accompanied a real hot looking cowboy dude out to his van," Steve said with a grin. "Fucking hot dude roped my wrists to the ceiling of the van and sucked me off two times. God almighty guys, never before has someone made me cum two times so soon... But I suppose I had to, seeing as he said he wouldn't release me until I had cum two times, ha!"

We quickly deduced that while Cleeve was dropping John off at my house Otis was busy sucking Steve's cock in the back of the van. But if he had Steve roped up as he said he was why didn't Otis kidnap the hunky bartender? Looking at Steve in all his musculature and massive bodied glory it was easy to tell that he was a Cleeve and Otis delight.

"Is the van still back there?" John asked Steve through clenched teeth. "A dark blue van?"

"Yeah, I think so," Steve said, still looking confused. "Fucking guy swallowed my load both times guys! FUCK!!"

We all stood silently for a brief moment...

"Uh, are you sure I didn't do anything wrong Officer?" Steve asked John, still taking in the sight of my buddies torn up uniform shirt and looking a tad more than worried now.

"Not at all Sir," John said and gently gave one of Steve's nipples a reassuring rub.

The cop then turned to look at me. By rubbing Steve's nipple John had just let the guy know in a subtle but clear way that he was definitely interested in him. Once again my leather bar had spawned another promising relationship...

"Kent, call Robinson down at headquarters, tell him to get a cruiser and two officers down here," John said, looking toward the back entrance of the bar. "Also, tell him that I'm okay."

"Where are you going?" I asked him as he started toward the back door.

"To finally bag those two bastards," John said to me, turning slightly. "Call Robinson, do as I asked you."

"But..." Bobby called out.

"And stay right in here Bobby," John said loudly, pointing a stern and rigid finger at my boy. "I have a bad fucking feeling it's you that they want again."

Bobby gulped hard and I quickly pulled him close to me... The boy's eyes rolled in his head and he broke out in a clammy sweat.

John stomped out to the deserted parking lot, hell bent on revenge for himself as well as Bobby. He checked his gun to be sure it was loaded and that the safety was off as he approached the infamous van, cautiously this time, checking behind him every few seconds for a lead pipe wielding Cleeve. While John went after Cleeve and Otis for the second time I made the call to Officer Robinson, my boy standing right by my side, a look of mortal fear etched on his handsome face... I decided then and there that Bobby would see my psychiatrist friend Doctor Andrew Carlson as soon as possible.

When John reached the back of the van he put his hand over the butt of his gun and with his other hand reached for the door handle.

"Fuckers," he whispered, turned the handle and yanked the van doors open.

The back of the van was dimly lit by one bulb hanging from the ceiling. The interior was deserted except for piles of rope, the bolts in the ceiling, the crate that those two fuckers had put Bobby in and the chair that was welded to the rugged floor of the van...

"Fuck, but they have to be here," John surmised softly. "They wouldn't just leave their van behind...or would they?"

Suddenly, from inside the crate John heard the sounds of "mmmmffff."

"Shit, they do have another victim in there already," the cop grunted angrily and hopped up into the back of the van. "Goddamned bastards..."

With two hands John threw open the top of the crate...

"Are you okay Sir?" John asked, without realizing who was in the crate.

Suddenly, Otis stood crouched upwards in the crate and before John could react or go for his gun Otis grabbed a handful of the cop's tattered shirt. He yanked John brutally forward...

"AACCHHH!!!" John panted as he was heaved forward and his shirt wrapped tightly around his neck.

Otis pointed a spray can at the cop's face, squeezed the plunger and sprayed a goodly amount of the can's contents, what smelled like some sort of nerve paralyzing gas in my buddies face. John tried to back away but Otis sprayed him again and John took another nose and mouth full of the stinking stuff...

"AAARRHHHHHH, GODS!!!" the cop gasped and fell to his knees in a stupor beside the crate as Otis climbed out of it.

Before loading John into the crate Otis handcuffed the cop, once again in his own cuffs and meanly sprayed another goodly amount of the gas in his face... The sounds of the van doors slamming shut and Otis calling out "mission accomplished" to Cleeve who was in the driver's seat sent a chill of fear that was indescribable up John's spine...

Just as the officer's that Robinson sent arrived Cleeve and Otis' van sped from the parking lot. The officers did not know to pursue the van as its owners took my good buddy Officer John McLaughlin with them yet again...

Part Four
(As told by Bobby's psychiatrist
Doctor Andrew Carlson)
(2007)

From Doctor Carlson's private journal: There's something so greatly attractive about a guy who has dark hair and sprinkles of grey at the temples. That's what Master Kent had. The first time I saw him at the leather bar I knew that I had to have him as my leather master. He told me that when our eyes met his heart accelerated to about a hundred miles per hour. I can honestly say mine did the same. Just the thought of his strong muscular arms around me, smothering me in the scent of his body mixed with his leathers was enough to send me over the edge. When he did hold me, when he trained me, when he loved and made love to me, my only thoughts were of pleasing him. My only true and deepest desire was his happiness...

When I knelt at his booted feet the tears that filled my eyes were tears of joy and of belonging. Master Kent embodied everything that I felt had been missing in my life since I was ten years old. He was father, leather master, mentor, confidant, teacher and lover.

He was also a very strict disciplinarian. Needless to say, that as his "boy" I suffered many paddlings, floggings and whippings at the hands of my loving master. He never disciplined me unnecessarily however... You see, I always came away having learned something...

-Related by Robert (also known as Bobby) Hollister in private therapy session-

It was twenty years ago at this point that my friend Master Kent brought his boy Bobby to me. It amazes even me that so many years have passed. It seems that time tends to speed up as we get older. Like Master Kent I had heard the stories about Cleeve and Otis, but I had not heard those stories by reading police reports as he had back in 1987, the same year his boy, Bobby, fell victim to the two serial kidnappers/rapists. I had heard the stories about Cleeve and Otis firsthand from Master Kent's boy Bobby himself. After Bobby's horrid experience of being kidnapped and repeatedly raped, beaten and humiliatingly abused to nearly within an inch of his young life Master Kent sent his boy to me for help. Because of what had been done to him at the hands of Cleeve and Otis Bobby was suffering recurring nightmares, sleep loss, sporadic meltdowns, loss of appetite, and he even passed out while at his construction job more than a few times. His co-workers reported seeing the young man break out in uncontrollable trembling, his eyes rolled and convulsed and then he was unconscious. The paramedics called to the scene reported that Bobby was suffering what is classically called post traumatic stress syndrome. Bobby finally agreed to put himself through therapy with me as his psychiatrist a few months after his experience. Through the years of intense therapy Bobby managed to not so much rid himself of the demons caused him by Cleeve and Otis, but he did find a way of putting the experience behind him and moving on with his life. I managed to show Bobby in our sessions that what had befallen him was no fault of his whatsoever. (Like many victims of kidnap and rape Bobby believed that what Cleeve and Otis had done to him was somehow his fault.) It was simply a horrid twist of events that had caused Bobby to become a victim of the men known as Cleeve and Otis. His relationship with Master Kent never suffered. That was the one thing that Bobby Hollister was always fervent about. Nothing, no man, no force of nature, nobody could break his love and devotion to his master. Now, twenty years later, sadly, Master Kent is gone, dead of a long bout with a recurring form of cancer that literally sapped his strength and his body. Bobby and I have remained good friends since he came to me for therapy and he has become a superb leather master himself, practically in Master Kent's image. He now owns the bar that Kent founded and proudly worked hard over the years to keep it a thriving business and success in his master's memory. Bobby proudly wears his master's leathers and at this point in time even has those distinguished looking grey sprinkles at his temples that he was so attracted to in Master Kent all those years ago. It always amazes me how Bobby has paid loving tribute to the man who changed his life both physically and mentally. A few years ago Bobby met a boy named Jack. At first he was reluctant to venture into a relationship. He felt that it would have been an insult to the memory of his loving master. We spoke about it and I advised Bobby that Master Kent would have wanted him to be happy. And not to mention how Bobby owed it to Master

Kent's memory to become a leather master with all the knowledge that had been bestowed upon him when he was a slave boy. When Bobby introduced Jack to me I was astonished at his resemblance to the beautifully breathtaking actor Leonardo DiCaprio. We all had a good laugh when I mentioned how he looked like the famous actor I just mentioned and how that actor had played a character named Jack in the Oscar winning movie, "Titanic." Bobby and Jack have been very happy together as master and slave boy. Jack is as devoted to Bobby as Bobby was to Master Kent. I often tell Bobby how proud of him Master Kent would have been. It's at those times when we are alone together that Bobby allows his tears to flow and his emotions to come to the surface. It breaks my heart to see the man cry over his lost master. Till this day, twenty years later he blames Cleeve and Otis for Master Kent's ruination. He also believes that if Cleeve and Otis hadn't kidnapped him back in 1987 Master Kent never would have harbored a rage so deep that Bobby believes brought on the cancer that eventually killed him. Through the nearly fifteen years that Bobby was in therapy with me and then when that doctor/patient relationship segued into the friendship we now share we had never heard anything more of the infamous Cleeve and Otis. We never learned what had become of Master Kent's cop buddy Officer John McLaughlin. It seemed that the ruggedly handsome cop that Cleeve and Otis had captured when he'd gone in pursuit of them the second time had literally vanished off the face of the earth. We never heard any other reports of men being abducted and tortured. We never heard anything until they resurfaced and claimed "me" as their victim. Twenty years after Bobby Hollister's abduction and tortures by Cleeve and Otis, I, Bobby's psychiatrist and friend would become their "final" victim... Remarkably enough I would also become Cleeve's sounding board...

As the first rosy pinks of the early morning rose over the horizon, a large dark blue van was making its way through the still dark streets of the deserted city...

"WHOOOOO WHEEEE, its quarry and twinkie time!!" Cleeve howled as he drove, sounding totally sadistic as his good buddy Otis smiled next to him, the two men in their new but ever infamous dark blue van. "Time for us to find a new mark for the night Otis my man!!"

"As you would say Cleeve, sure as shit, sure as fucking shit," Otis said gleefully, his eyes peeled and watching out the van windows for some lone guy, a leftover perhaps from the party circuit of the night before foolish enough to be walking the streets during the wee hours of the night, or perhaps as some thought of it, the wee hours of the morning.

It was Sunday, February 25th, 2007 and New York City was freezing. The two men known only as Cleeve and Otis did not look as if twenty years has passed since they abducted Master Kent's boy, Bobby and meanly followed it up by abducting the leather master's good buddy Officer John McLaughlin. The scar that is etched deep on the right side of Otis' face, a scraggly line reaching from under his ear-lobe stretching down to his chin is the only truly distinctive difference marking the passage of twenty years time. That scar and perhaps a few gray hairs here and there for the two mysterious night crawlers.

"So what are you in the mood to feast on tonight?" Otis asked as Cleeve drove along the quiet streets. "Some succulent and tender boy meat perhaps or maybe a rugged soldier boy? I know that there's an after hours bar not far from here where a lot of military brats hang out."

As Otis spoke Cleeve found himself simply staring aimlessly through the windshield as he drove.

"Something wrong man?" Otis asked, noticing the look of uncertainty in his good buddies' eyes.

"We've done it all haven't we Otis?" Cleeve asked with a smirk on his face.

"What do you mean?" Otis asked in reply.

"Boy meat, soldier boys, that marine we managed to capture while he was here in New York City on vacation, man how he squealed every time his ass was porked, construction dudes, fuck man, remember that construction worker we snagged?" Cleeve laughed. "If I remember right his name was Paul. Oh man, remember how we tied that fucker to the post at his jobsite and nearly sucked his tits right off his chest? HAH!! Fucking guy swore at us that if we didn't leave his tits alone he would make short work of us! HA! And of all things we left him there tied to that fucking post all the live long night! I would bet any fucking amount of money that when his work buddies showed up that morning and found him tied up like that they couldn't resist having at his tits a bit before they released him! HA! Fucking Paul man had tits better than any woman alive! And what about that police rookie? Fucking shit man, that poor sap didn't think we'd ever let him go! HA!!! And that rock and roll stud we landed! Oh man, when we charged those elites of high society to have at him, fuck, we walked away with thousands of dollars that time! The entire world adored that fucking rock and roller stud and we sold his ass like he was some cheap whore!! I'm getting a hard-on just remembering that suave guy when he begged us to let him go! Remember how we bagged him in his dressing room after his show Otis? He told us how his bodyguards would get us for what we were doing to him! HA! And when he saw his bodyguards all tied up outside his dressing room as we lugged him off like a sack of dirty laundry, man oh fucking man did he screech and beg through that gag! They all begged Otis, every fucking last one of them…they all begged… And Larry, oh man, HA!!! Fucking Soldier Brown, twice, twice we nailed that fucking soldier boy, even though he claimed he was only out playing war games with his corporate buddies! How he went on about how he wasn't a real soldier when we lugged him to our van…yeah Otis, we've done it all and then some…and they never caught us for it…"

"How can you forget that master's boy we caught? Remember him?" Otis asked and touched the scar on his face.

"Yeah, *how* can we forget him?" Cleeve asked agreeably. "Fucking sweet boy he was! Bobby his name was, Master Kent's boy…"

"Yeah, Master Kent…" Otis said and trailed a fingertip down the scar on his face.

Cleeve took a deep breath, licked his lips and then said, "And his buddy, Officer Stupid McLaughlin…"

As the two men drove aimlessly in search of fresh prey Bobby and I were at that very moment not all that far away from Cleeve and Otis' van. Bobby, now forty two years old, totally muscular in his late master's image, his dark eyes still piercing and seductive was just leaving my office alongside me as I locked up the front door.

"I can't believe we stayed up talking just about all night Dr. Carlson," Bobby said to me, his hands crammed deep in his jacket pockets as he fought the cold night air. "I'm sorry I took up so much of your time…"

I smiled at him, the "boy" that had meant life to my late friend Master Kent and told him that he had not taken up my time at all. I gently patted him on the back, told him that he needed to talk and that as his therapist and friend that was what I was there for.

"It's why Master Kent referred you to me all those years ago Bobby," I said, giving the front of his jacket a tug. "I'm always here for you…"

"*Master Kent…*" Bobby said softly and as usual as he spoke his leather masters name his beautiful eyes filled with tears. "You know Doctor Carlson; I still can't believe that nearly ten years have gone by since he died of cancer… Even after all this time there are times that I still can't believe he's gone…"

"I know Bobby," I said and put an arm around the young man as we stood, still talking in front of my office.
We were both freezing but somehow we were not aware of that fact.

"But you know that he's really not gone if you keep him alive in your heart and soul," I said to Bobby as I held him. "And I know that the way he loved you he's always with you…boy…"

Bobby let his tears flow and snuffed heartily in the cold air. His face lit up in a smile mixed with tears and he giggled like a teenager when I referred to him as "boy", his former status in the leather world. As I held him and let him cry once more for his lost master I recalled how when he first came to me Bobby swore that he did not need therapy. But when the nightmares didn't cease, when the meltdowns became more frequent and his appetite suffered and when he passed out at work was when Master Kent put his (booted) foot down and made him come to see me. It was the best thing Master Kent ever did for his boy. Over the years I assisted Bobby in dealing with his demons, but Master Kent's demons were much more below the surface it seemed than Bobby's were. His demon, one called revenge would not be sated until he'd made Cleeve and Otis pay in some way for what they had done to the boy he had been so miraculously blessed with…

As Bobby and I stood in front of my office saying our long "good-night's" he looked at me through his tear-filled eyes and said, "I can still remember how he looked that night after he had found Cleeve and Otis down at the waterfront, all those years after they had captured me. It seemed that over the years they favored that sleazy area for some of their marks. Master Kent came home battered but triumphant looking. He told me how he had nailed those two bastards for what they had done to me but he was anguished still the same, seeing as no matter what they wouldn't tell him what they'd done with Officer John McLaughlin.
Bobby shivered in the cold night air and went on, saying, "We never found out what became of the cop."

"Someday we might Bobby," I said and looked at my watch.

"Now, you have a boy to get home to."

At the mention of his boy, Jack, Bobby's tear-filled eyes lit up and he smiled widely...

"Yeah, he's probably thinking that I ran off and had an affair," Bobby chuckled and I laughed along with him.

"How are things between the two of you?" I asked.

"Very good I must say, he learns fast, and I'm enjoying training him," Bobby said. "Actually, I'm training him in the same ways that Master Kent trained me. He's very devoted to me."

I smiled and said, "Master Kent taught you well Bobby, he would have been proud."

At that we hugged one more time and Bobby said, "Have a good night my friend."

"You too," I said as he kissed me on the cheek before walking to his car, which was parked right behind mine.

As I finished locking up my office Bobby drove off. While Bobby and I had been standing and talking in front of my office neither of us had taken notice of the dark blue van as it had made its way up the street. I suppose it could be said that we were too wrapped up in our conversation and shivering from the cold as well to pay attention to much else.

"Well, well, would you looky there Otis?" Cleeve said as he took in the sight of Bobby and me, him not recognizing Bobby at first. "Two to choose from, one a handsome and regal looking suit and tie and the other a construction worker dude...some contrast those two huh? I wonder what the fuck would bring two such different types together..."

"Fuck me but that construction worker dude looks familiar Cleeve," Otis said as he peered out the window, his heart racing. "Oh holy fuck, do you know who that construction guy is Cleeve?" That's Master Kent's boy, that's Bobby! Holy fuck, he may look a bit older but that's him! All these years and there he is!! Shit, we got to snag him Cleeve, that way I'll finally have my revenge on that leather master of his for what he did to me..." As Otis railed he again fingered the scar on his cheek... Cleeve, only half paying attention to Otis quickly pulled the van over, doused the headlights and peered over at Bobby and me as we finished our conversation outside my office...

"I think I want the blond suit and tie Otis," Cleeve said softly, staring into his side mirror, watching as Bobby and I began to part ways, him walking to his car and me turning to finish locking up my office.

"The blond suit and tie?" Otis echoed as Cleeve took in the sight of me as I turned the key in the lock. "Cleeve, we can get a blond suit and tie any fucking day of the week! But Bobby? Master Kent's boy?" How often is that going to be dropped in our laps?"

As Otis went on and on Bobby drove off, passing right by the infamous pair's van, waving a final "good-bye" to me as I turned and headed toward my car.

"I said I want the blond suit and tie Otis," Cleeve said, turning and looking at his cohort through steely eyes. "Don't you see that sign hanging on the front lawn of that house that looks like it was made into an office?"

Otis looked where Cleeve was pointing and saw the sign that read, "Andrew Carlson, MD., Psychiatrist. He looked at Cleeve and said, "So the suit and tie is a psychiatrist, what of it?"

"All that talk back there of all those men we snagged Otis," Cleeve said. "I want to explore Otis, I want to explore myself. Like you said just now, twenty years...*twenty* fucking years since we snagged that boy Bobby and then we see him in front of a shrink's office! It's like fate man, you mention him and then there he is! I've been thinking about it man, I want to explore...myself..."

Otis looked at his longtime buddy in complete disbelief.

"Cleeve, you mean to say you want to kidnap that psychiatrist and tell him about your past?" Otis asked. "Fuck man, talk to me, I'll listen...I've known you all these years. I've been by your side through all of it! Talk to me man, I'm always here for you Cleeve!"

Cleeve mulled that over for a second as he watched me making my way toward my car...

"Thanks for the offer Otis, but we've known each other too long for something like that," Cleeve replied. "No, this is fate, seeing that shrink with Master Kent's boy, while we were talking about him at that, and now there he is...its like fate..." Cleeve said and gripped the steering wheel tighter. "I want the blond suit and tie..."

As I started across the street I reached into the pocket of my overcoat for my car keys... At the same moment Cleeve gunned the ignition of the van and moved from the parking space, his headlights hugely luminous as he drove directly toward me...

"WHAT THE???" I barked loudly, stupidly stopping dead in the middle of the street as the van plowed toward me.

Holding up my hands I felt like a deer caught in the headlights of an oncoming car. Cleeve swerved to avoid hitting me, narrowly evaded side swiping me and in my terror I dropped my car keys. I spun around involuntarily as the van came to a halt beside me.

"Good evening Sir, or perhaps in your case it's good morning," Otis said to me, leering down at me from his perch in the passenger seat.

When I saw the scar on the man's face I instantly knew who I was in the presence of ...

"My partner and I seem to have lost our way and we were wondering if you could possibly help us out with some directions..." Otis said, smiling evilly down at me as he spoke.

"H-holy cr-crap..." I said as my mind spun with the unreality of this.

As I was about to back away from the van and run for my life it was at that moment that Otis pushed the passenger side door open, slamming me with it, hard and bodily.

"HOOOFFFFF!!!" was the sound I made as the door connected with my torso and I found myself stumbling backward on my wing-tipped feet, my arms flailing in front of me.

I hit the pavement on my back with my legs splayed embarrassingly upwards in the air for a moment.

"*Oh my God...*" I whispered in mortal fear and as I sat up my head spun.

I saw Otis climbing down out of the van and making his way toward me. Backing up on the palms of my hands and the heels of my shoes I looked around the deserted street for help, *any kind of help.* The way I had been struck with the van door had my head spinning and I knew there wasn't much I was going to be able to do to defend myself. There wasn't even a homeless person to be found let alone a cop. I spied my car not all that far away and as I tried to get to my feet Otis kicked out a foot and toppled me back down to the ground.

"UHHHNNFFF!!!" I grunted as I again hit the ground on my back.

I saw Cleeve at the back of their infamous van, opening the doors... It was at that moment, based on Bobby's tale of abduction at the hands of these two men all those years ago, that I knew they were going to kidnap me…

"So Doctor Carlson, are you the boy's shrink?" Otis teased me, looking meanly down at me as I looked up at him in mortal fear.

"You leave that guy alone or I swear I'll…" I seethed as I pulled myself up on my elbows, ready to somehow do battle with the oaf-like looking stack of muscles that Otis was.

"You'll what?" Otis chortled, reached down and grabbed my ankles.

As he yanked me forward and lifted me by my ankles I snarled at him to let go of me, ranting loudly, praying that someone would hear me and call the police. Cleeve made his way over to us and grabbed my flailing arms… As I struggled fruitlessly in their grasps the two men lugged me to their van. The opened back doors of that van looked to me like a giant mouth of some kind that was ready to swallow me up whole… I thought of all the other men who had come before me and who had been abducted in like fashion. I wondered what those men had thought as they were loaded into the van by Cleeve and Otis.

"FUCK, FUCK!!! HELP ME!!! OH GOD SOMEONE HELP ME!!!" I bellowed awfully as I was tossed into the back of the back of the vehicle. "UHHHHNNFFF…"

It didn't take all that long for the two expert kidnappers to get me restrained in a tight and confining hogtie… As they hogtied me I saw the crate that Bobby had mentioned being put in for his ride to Cleeve's infamous house of horrors. I whispered the words "My God" over and over at the sight of that crate. I saw the bolts in the ceiling and on the floor of the van where no doubt men taken prisoner had been confined for their ride to wherever Cleeve and Otis bring their prey. The past was telling me its secrets through the interior of the vehicle. The two men quickly tied me up, gagged and blindfolded me and left me alone in the back of the van. A few moments later I heard the maniacal laughter from the front seat of the vehicle as the van started moving…

"GGGRRMMFFFFFF!!!!" I wailed helplessly.

As the van was driven away the only clue as to what had happened to me was my car keys where I had dropped them on the ground…

As Bobby had told me in our sessions, from his estimates, and now mine, the drive to Cleeve's house took better than two hours. And let me tell you that that length of time is awful to keep a poor guy hogtied... My arms and legs were beyond numb by the time we arrived at wherever the two men had brought me to...

When the van came to a halt I heard the two men disembark and then the back doors were thrown open.

"MMMFFFFFFF!!!" I railed at my two captors as I heard them step up into the interior of my present prison.

"Hope you enjoyed the ride Doc," Cleeve said, whipped the blindfold off me and as my vision cleared I saw him looking down lecherously at me.

From what I had heard of Cleeve and Otis from Bobby and from what we knew of the police reports on Cleeve and Otis and the kind of men they favored for their escapades it didn't make sense that they had kidnapped me. All the men that the infamous pair had snagged for their sadistic pleasures were well built and younger than me, ranging in the age group between early twenties to mid thirties. I was what would be called on the lanky side and I was in my very late forties... What was it they wanted from me? If they planned on torturing me the way they had done to Bobby all those years ago I would be dead in no time...

"MMMMFFFF!!!" was all I could say in reply as the two men towered over me.

"Lets get him inside Otis, the doctor has a long night ahead of him," Cleeve said and I frantically shook my head "no" from side to side as they untied me from the hogtie, leaving my hands bound behind me.

A few minutes later I found myself standing between the two men in front of Cleeve's huge sprawling house. It was huge, sort of like the old plantation homes dating back to the 1800's. As I took in the sight of the house Otis took the gag out of my mouth.

"Feeling okay Doc?" Cleeve asked and squeezed the back of my neck. "May I say that you're the first doctor to ever be brought here to my home?"

"Wh-what the fuck?" I said softly, not believing my own ears, hearing myself swear, something I rarely do. "Why have you done this??? Why have you kidnapped me? If you think for a second that by torturing me you're going to get your sick jollies you're wasting your goddamned time!"

"Ah well, we'll just see about that," Otis said as the two men held me by my upper arms and started moving me toward the huge mansion-like house.

The house actually looked beautiful and inviting in the early morning sun the way it was located by itself on the road and surrounded by nothing but woods. But it was what the house had on the inside of it that made it ugly, from what I had heard about through the reports. And the woods mocked me because I knew that they were the sight of the awful tortures that Bobby had endured all those years ago...

Cleeve and Otis brought me into the house and scurried me quickly down to a basement three levels below the ground. The basement was actually a dungeon of sorts, adorned with medieval looking devices of torture. I wondered if this was where they had first brought Bobby years ago. Cleeve left me standing with Otis while he went into one of the rooms of the basement. Standing there with my hands tied behind me there wasn't all that much that I could do as the man with horrid looking scar on his face extracted my wallet from the front pocket of my suit jacket.

"Doctor Andrew Carlson eh?" Otis asked me and tugged at my tie.
He rummaged through my wallet and found the usual stash of credit cards, a driver's license and a small amount of cash.

"So what's your connection to Master Kent's boy Bobby?" he asked me. "We saw you standing and talking with him in front of your office before we snagged your ass..."

"That's none of your damned business!" I spat in response and Otis backhanded me across the face for my nasty response, the sound of the slap echoing in the basement/dungeon. "UUHHHFFFFFF!!!!"

I toppled backward and landed with my back against a concrete post. As my head spun once again from being struck by Otis I glanced to my sides and saw the metal manacles welded into the post I had landed against.

"*Shit...*" I panted as Otis approached me, a look of utter insanity in his eyes, the scar on his cheek making his look all the more demonic somehow.

"I'll ask you one more time Doc," Otis said, reaching for me.

Suddenly, from behind Otis we heard the words, "Otis, stop, that's enough..."

We both looked behind where Otis was standing and saw Cleeve coming out of the room he had gone into. He was carrying a wooden straight backed chair and some rope was draped over his shoulder.

"Enough?" Otis asked Cleeve. "Fuck man, we haven't even gotten started on this shrink..."

I cowered against the post as Otis grabbed the lapels of my suit jacket and nearly lifted me out of my shoes as he pulled me away from the structure.

"Otis lets just get him stripped down to his underwear and tied to this chair for today," Cleeve said. "We can decide by tonight what the hell we're going to do with him..."

I could tell from the tone of Cleeve's voice that he was merely humoring his cohort. Somehow I got the feeling that Cleeve didn't intend to torture me. I, like Otis, had to wonder about that. What the hell *was* going on here?

Holding me by the lapels in a firm grip, the tips of my shoes dangling over the floor Otis looked to Cleeve and said, "You were really serious back there in the van weren't you?" I glanced at the men from side to side and wondered what Otis meant. The next thing I knew my hands were untied and I was being unceremoniously stripped of my suit...

A short while later I was bound to the straight backed chair, wearing just my white boxer briefs. I felt totally humiliated being put on display in such a fashion...

"Okay Cleeve, as you said, by tonight we can decide what to do with this handsome fucking doctor, but after we're done with him I want at Master Kent's boy again..." Otis said sternly.

"NO, NO!!!!" I railed up at Otis as he stood over me, my tie and socks dangling in one of his hands. "Leave that guy alone! You two have no idea what he's endured in his life!!!"

Otis pursed his lips together, threw his free hand back and whapped me again good and hard across the face.

"AARRHHHH!!!" I bellowed miserably as my head snapped back and then forward again.

"What he endured?" Otis snarled at me, dropping my tie and socks to the floor. "Look at my face Doctor Stupid!! Do you see what I've endured??? That boy's master did this to me and..."

"And that boy's master is dead you sick fuck!!" I ranted and Otis belted me again across the cheek. "YUHHHHHHHH!!!!"

At my last words Cleeve's jaw seemed to drop and he grabbed Otis' wrist, holding the man back as he was about to again crack me across the face. My head was spinning in a reverse sort of orbit and I could feel the stinging marks of the imprint that Otis' fingers had left on my face.

"Kent is dead?" Cleeve asked.

"Y-yes, yes," I stammered, my head hanging down as I sat there in my underpants. "Dead of cancer…"

Cleeve let go of Otis' wrist and the big oaf whacked me yet again.

"UHHHNNNN…" I gasped and Otis gave me yet another. "UUHHFFFFFFF!!!!"

"I'll tell you Doc, that's just a sample of what I plan to give you after my buddy here is done with you…" Otis said sneering at me as he leaned down menacingly over the chair I was bound to. "In Master Kent's memory I'll scar that boy's face just like he did to mine!!"

"Over my dead body you'll hurt that young man again…" I began and when Otis raised his hand again I pulled my head back.

I was shocked however when he suddenly knelt in front of me, reached into the fly opening of my underpants and brought out my semi hard cock and big floppy balls.

"OHHHHHHRRR FUCK, easy with my manhood you bastard," I railed as Otis didn't handle me all that gently down there.

To further my shock I was breathless as Otis gobbled my cock into his mouth and began sucking it.

"OOOHHHHHHHHH…" I moaned and writhed under the tight ropes as the guy expertly sucked me up to a man-sized erection.

Otis squeezed my balls a few times as he sucked me harder and harder, his lips and tongue playing a tune called ecstasy on my skin flute…

It didn't take all that long before I was spewing a hearty gusher in the sadistic guy's mouth. Cleeve simply stood by watching as his buddy ate my jazz.

"AAAAAARRRHHH," I grunted loudly as I seemed to cum and cum. "Bastard, what kind of shit is this, rap a guy across the face till his head is spinning and then siphon his juices from him???"

I was feeling a mixture of pain and sheer ecstasy as I was sucked even as I shot my load, seemingly endlessly down Otis' gullet. When I was done he slowly let my manhood slip from his mouth, his lips smacking it delicately as it left his craw.

"Now I can sleep on a full stomach," Otis said as he got to his feet. "That was just a sample of what you're in for Doc…"

Otis told Cleeve that he was feeling tired, seeing as he hadn't slept well the day before and that he was going to get some rest. I had to wonder. It sounded like these two men slept days and spent their nights wandering the streets of the city in search of prey. Cleeve told his cohort that that was a good idea. Otis looked at me fiendishly and then left the basement/dungeon, his big booted feet stomping up the stairs as he went.

"As you can see my buddy is hell bent on revenge where that master's boy is concerned," Cleeve said to me as I sat there with my cock and balls still on display outside my underpants.

"Can I get you something to drink Doctor Carlson?" Cleeve asked me and as I looked at the godlike man I could not believe that this was the same man who had tortured Bobby and then kidnapped Officer McLaughlin all those years ago.

"I'm a scotch and water man myself," I replied miserably, glancing down at my cock as the last remnants of my jazz dribbled from my slit. "But I doubt you would have that sort of drink down here in a dungeon..."

"You are incorrect Doctor Carlson, I have everything down here," Cleeve said and again left the room, but this time leaving me on my own rather than with Otis.

I struggled mightily under the binding ropes but it was no use. I was tied too tight. There was no way I could get myself free. I would simply have to deal with whatever the two men had in store for me. Looking across the room at the device called a "rack" that dominated the room I shuddered. I thought of how Master Kent had used the rack in a loving manner to train his boy whereas I had no doubt that Cleeve and Otis used it to torture their victims to a state of mind called madness...

Cleeve returned a short time later with a small glass of scotch and water... He pulled a chair up across from the one I was sitting in. As he fed me the amber liquid I sipped it slowly and he gave my cock a squeeze or two.

"You have to excuse Otis, but you're the first man we've encountered in years who has any connection to Master Kent's boy, Bobby..." Cleeve said to me when I'd stopped drinking.

"I excuse nothing when it comes to the two of you," I replied angrily. "That young man is..."

"Yeah, we know, one of the kindest and gentlest persons on

the planet..." Cleeve said, finishing my sentence for me. "So we were told..."

"He suffered enough growing up and his true joy in finding Master Kent was a godsend for him," I said. "Then you two came along and kidnapped him...and..."

Cleeve interrupted my repertoire to ask what I meant about how Bobby had suffered while growing up. I supposed that there really was no harm in Cleeve knowing some of Bobby's sad past. In fact I hoped that it would somehow touch whatever heart the man had. I told of how when Bobby was ten years old his parents, his dad a United States marine sergeant and his mom a loving wife were senselessly killed in a car accident.

"They had attended a military social gathering and were on their way home when a group of drunken teenagers in another car slammed into their car and accidentally shoved them off the road," I said to Cleeve. "Bobby's father was driving. From what was gathered at the scene of the horrid accident it was decreed that the marine tried to control the car, but once he had been driven off the road and the car was plunging down the ravine it was too late. The car exploded in a ball of fire and Bobby's parents were gone..."

Cleeve looked at me and I swore that I could almost see regret in his eyes...for perhaps a split second or two. He asked me what had become of the drunken teenagers in the car that had run Bobby's parents off the road. I told him how they were still serving jail time till this day.

"Bobby lived with his Uncle Charlie, his dad's younger brother till he was twenty or so," I went on. "He started working for the construction company "Green and Sons" as soon as he graduated high school. Bobby had no time or the money for college so he simply went to work as a construction worker. He became one of the youngest supervisors the company ever had. He worked hard; he broke his back so that he could afford the things he wanted. It wasn't long after he became a crew supervisor that he met Master Kent. And the rest as they say is history."

Cleeve pursed his lips together, fed me some more of the scotch and water and as I sipped I saw regret in his eyes, this time I was sure of it.

"So the kid worked for Green and Sons Construction, that's rich, that's real rich," Cleeve said and that glint of sadism returned to his eyes.

I asked what he meant by that and he said that at the moment it really didn't matter, but that he would tell me later, when the time was right. In turn Cleeve asked me if Bobby still worked for Green and Sons, although somehow I got the feeling that he knew he didn't.

"After Master Kent died Bobby became the owner of the leather bar that Kent owned," I said. "He also owns the house they lived in. So no, Bobby no longer works for Green and Sons."

"Jeez man, I can't believe Master Kent is dead," Cleeve said and stood up, leaned over me to feed me the rest of my scotch and water and with the empty glass in hand leaned against a post, seeming to be taking in the sight of my cock and balls as they hung out of my underpants. "You said it was cancer?"

"Yes, a very rare and fast moving form of stomach cancer," I said.

I told Cleeve how the symptoms had started in April of 1998 and by November of that same year the man that Bobby had loved for a little more than ten years was gone. Master Kent was starting to lose his appetite a little at a time. He was never one not to finish a hearty meal. After that he complained how foods didn't taste right to him, thinking that perhaps the food had gone bad before he or Bobby had cooked it. The stomach pains came not all that long after his food would taste strange to him. Bobby pleaded with his master to go to the doctor for some tests. He saw that Kent was already losing weight and that his pallor was turning pasty and pale looking. When Master Kent asked Bobby to run the bar for him a few nights a week was when Bobby knew that something was dreadfully wrong with the man he loved. Master Kent loved that bar. It was a reflection of the success he had dreamed of. He hated being away from that bar as much as he hated being away from Bobby. For Master Kent his boy and his bar were the two things he loved most in this world. They both filled him with love and pride. One night when Bobby got home from the bar he found Master Kent in the bathroom. The man was doubled over, over the toilet and vomiting uncontrollably. By then he had lost nearly fifteen pounds. Bobby saw that the toilet was filled with whatever Master Kent had managed to eat that day and blood. More than anything there was blood that Kent had spewed as he vomited. When he heard Bobby say "Master Kent, oh my God!" he reached for the toilet handle and flushed away the mess. It was at that moment that Bobby took control. He told

Master Kent he was going to the hospital whether he wanted to or not. The leather master did not argue as Bobby dialed 911 and requested an ambulance to their address post haste. Master Kent was rushed to the hospital and after two days of tests his doctor told him and Bobby the dreadful, awful news. Master Kent had stomach cancer. To make his situation all the worse it was a rare form of stomach cancer and there wasn't much that could be done for him other than to make the man as comfortable as possible for his time that remained. Bobby was stalwart and strong as they listened. He held his master's frail hand in his as the doctor explained the death sentence.
"And just how much time are we looking at here Doctor?" Master Kent asked the doctor, speaking softly because even talking could hurt for him at that point.

The doctor said that it was so difficult to make that kind of determination but it was Bobby who managed to extract the information from him. Holding his master's hand and choking on his tears of rage Bobby clenched his teeth and said, "My master asked you a question. You will respect him by answering him, no matter how difficult the truth is!" Master Kent smiled lovingly at his boy and squeezed his hand. The doctor looked at the two men quizzically and then realized the relationship they shared. He apologized to Bobby and said that the most he figured on was five months. Bobby squeezed his master's hand tighter and managed to hold his tears. Master Kent lasted seven months, he was that strong... After the doctor left the two men alone Master Kent told Bobby that he was going to get some sleep and for the boy to go home. Bobby insisted that he wanted to stay but when Master Kent gave an order the boy obeyed, always. The boy always obeyed his master. As Bobby kissed Kent on the cheek the leather master told his boy that he was proud of him for how he had just wrested the information from the doctor. Through his tears as they filled his eyes Bobby whispered, "I love you Master Kent," and he left the room...

As fate would have it I happened to be at the hospital that day visiting with another friend of mine who had been admitted for an upcoming operation, nothing serious. I saw Bobby as he was coming out of Kent's room. Needless to say the boy was in tears. I called out to him as he walked down the hall in the opposite direction from me. When he turned and saw me he simply threw out his arms to me and sobbed. He sobbed so pitifully. I held him as tight as possible as he told me the horrible news. I managed to get him to the lounge and calm him a bit. I let his tears of sorrow and rage flow as I held him and he shook uncontrollably in my arms. I whispered that I was there for him, that he would get through this. He was a strong man and his master had taught him well, I reminded him of those things. His wails of agony broke my heart, knowing how he'd grown up minus his parents. When he finally calmed down he thanked me and I drove him home. I needed to keep my emotions in check for Bobby. I felt just as awful as he did, seeing as Master Kent had been one of my closest and dearest friends for many years...

He died in November, seven months after he had been diagnosed with cancer. Bobby was there when it happened. Kent was very doped up on Morphine; the pain had gotten that ghastly. Half the time he didn't even know that Bobby was there, but on that last day he knew. Somehow he managed to climb up out of the Morphine stupor. He was holding Bobby's hand in his skeletal like hand and when Bobby heard his name whispered he looked at his master through tear filled eyes. Bobby's tears flowed silently as Master Kent whispered, "My boy, my beautiful, beautiful boy, how I love you Bobby. I love you so much. I loved you the moment I saw you and I will love you for all eternity. You have made me so happy! No leather master was ever so blessed as I was to have had you in my life." Bobby snuffed and held his master's hand just a tad tighter, not wanting to hurt him. He told Kent not to talk but the leather master insisted that he had to, he just had to. Kent went on, whispering, practically heaving out his last words to his beloved. "Don't be alone Bobby. Remember the things I taught you. It's now your responsibility to pass that along. Be happy my boy! You have so much love in you to offer. Don't waste it, don't waste it. Please be happy. You will be a leather master Bobby, but you will ALWAYS be my boy Bobby, always *my* boy..."

Bobby let out a pitiful sob and gathered his master into his arms. He held Kent tight and sobbed awfully. When the nurse came in and told Bobby that Kent was gone he yelled at her to get out and to leave them alone for a while. When she saw the distraught and broken hearted young man she complied with his wishes. I stood at Bobby's side at the funeral ceremony when we buried his master. The young man sobbed more over the loss of the man he called "Master" than over how he had been tortured by Cleeve and Otis.

Cleeve looked at me and I could tell that from what I had just related to him that his heart broke for Bobby. Somehow I had gotten inside the man. He was human after all and there was something there that had just touched his heart.

"And you monsters tortured that boy," I seethed at him through my own tears that had flowed as I related the story of Master Kent's death. "Do you know what that did to Kent to know how you had hurt Bobby?"

"Yeah, actually I do know," Cleeve replied. "The scar that you saw on Otis' face was given to him by Master Kent."

I already knew that story, of how Cleeve and Otis had attempted to abduct Master Kent but found him to be a better than worthy adversary, a lot better than all the men they had abducted put together. But even though I already knew it I wanted to hear it now from Cleeve's side. He sat back down and told me how a few years after he and Otis had abducted Bobby and then had had Officer John McLaughlin worked over at the sleazy bar called "The Local" they had returned there looking for fresh prey, as they called the men they hunted in the wee hours of the day. "The Local" always attracted the sleaziest types of men it seemed. On the night that Cleeve and Otis were there looking once again for a new mark it was Otis who heard someone call out the name "Master Kent." It seemed that the leather master was there with police officer Robinson, both of them trying to find any clues or information that might have led to the whereabouts of the still missing Officer John McLaughlin. Otis saw Master Kent and Officer Robinson talking to the bartender at "The Local." Both Kent and the police officer looked sickened when it was told to them of how Officer McLaughlin had been repeatedly raped and worked over in the bar only a few months prior. But since then no one had seen him…

Otis quickly pointed Master Kent out to Cleeve and the two men decided to make him their next victim. They returned to their van and waited patiently outside the sleazy bar for Master Kent to emerge. When they saw Officer Robinson drive off in his police cruiser without Kent they knew that their chances of snagging the rugged leather master had just increased tenfold. Cleeve told me they waited till nearly closing time for Kent to leave "The Local." I knew that the reason Kent stayed there was that he was hoping for his cop buddy to suddenly make an appearance there, seeing as it had been the scene of the crime when he had been kidnapped. Kent had no doubt that the officer would have wanted to arrest each and every one of the men who had participated in his rape and degradations. At four AM when Officer

McLaughlin hadn't magically appeared the bar emptied out and by 4:30 AM Kent left as well, the area around "The Local" now deserted. It was a prime moment for Cleeve and Otis to make their move. The two men sat in their van as Master Kent walked right past it, headed for his car. As Kent headed for his car he heard the van doors open and then close behind him. He turned at the sound of Otis calling out, "Master Kent!" Kent turned and standing under a lamppost looked totally statuesque and magnificent in all his musculature and leather. When Kent saw the two men approaching him he knew instantly who they were. He swore under his breath and images of what had been done to Bobby played in his mind like a horror movie.

"Where's my friend? Where is Officer John McLaughlin?" Kent asked the two men through clenched teeth.

"Who? Officer Who?" Cleeve asked the leather master mockingly. "Tell me Master Kent, how's that succulent boy of yours doing these days? He about ready for another good go round with Otis and me?"

"You sons of bitches, I'll kill the two of you for what you did to Bobby," Kent railed and as Cleeve and Otis suddenly rushed at him he jammed his huge hands into meaty fists.

Cleeve took the first blow that Master Kent threw, right across his jaw. Cleeve let out a howling grunt of pain as he spun back and slammed bodily against Kent's parked car. While his attention had been on Cleeve Kent didn't see Otis about to try to pummel him from behind. As the leather master turned he saw Otis standing with both hands raised into a giant fist. No one knew that Kent was, besides a rugged leather master, a black-belt in karate. As Otis' hands came down, about to pound Master Kent on the spine the leather man kicked out his right foot and the bottom of his boot connected hard with Otis' knees, sending the man sprawling to the pavement. Like Cleeve had just done seconds before Otis let out a loud wail of pain. Master Kent heard Cleeve say, "You'll pay for that Master Kent" as he managed to capture the leather master in a headlock from behind. Kent made choking sounds as Cleeve tightened his arm-grip around his neck, backing him up toward their infamous van.

"Your boy rode in our van, your cop buddy rode in our van, and now it's your turn you fucking stud," Cleeve whispered in Kent's ear, slurping at his lobe as he spoke, all the while Kent trying with his fingers and thumbs to free Cleeve's arm from around his neck. "And I'm willing to bet a million fucking smackers that you'll be better than your boy and that cop put together…"

As Cleeve inched the leather master toward the van Otis got to his feet, his knees still wobbly.

"I wonder how that succulent boy of yours will feel when he finds out that we got you now," Cleeve taunted Kent, sucking his earlobe in between speaking. "You think maybe he'll be jealous Master Kent?"

As Cleeve snickered and Otis followed behind him Kent clenched his teeth, yelled out an earsplitting "FUCK YOU!!!" and stomped a booted foot hard on one of Cleeve's feet, causing Cleeve to lose his arm-hold on Kent… Once more Cleeve ranted in pain. Master Kent turned quickly and once more gave Cleeve a hard fist across the jaw. Otis screamed along with Cleeve as two teeth and blood flew from Cleeve's mouth. Cleeve landed in back of his van in a heap. It was at that moment that Otis pulled the knife, standing there pointing it at Kent as the leather man once more approached him.

"I'll kill you man, I swear I will," Otis railed, brandishing the long sharp teethed knife. "I never killed anyone Kent, don't be the first!! Just back off!!"

"Why should I back off you scum?" Kent seethed, rubbing the sore spot on his neck where Cleeve had strangle-held him just moments before, his breathing sounding more like rasping sounds. "You two attacked me! And now you want me to back off! You two did unimaginable things to my boy, and now you want me to back off! Where the fuck is my cop buddy???"

As Otis suddenly lunged forward with the knife pointed at Kent Cleeve looked up from the ground. He saw Kent kick out again, this time his booted foot connecting with Otis' midsection. Otis dropped the knife but Kent caught it by the handle before it hit the ground. Cleeve felt as if he was now watching the spectacle battle between Otis and Master Kent in slow motion. As Otis looked up Kent screamed out in a man's agony, "YOU SCUM, you almost killed my boy!!!" and swung the knife forward toward Otis. As Otis looked up the knife came down across his face, digging in deep under his ear and then Kent brought it sliding down the side of the man's face, Kent screaming, "That's for Bobby you bastard!!" Cleeve screamed Otis' name and more blood spewed from where his teeth had been that Kent had literally knocked out. Blood, now from Otis' face splattered on the pavement. As Master

Kent made his way to his car, taking Otis' knife with him he watched for a moment as the two men huddled with each other and he heard Cleeve saying that the cut was too deep, that they had to get Otis medical attention instantly. Kent, sitting in the driver's seat of his car watched as Cleeve helped Otis into their van and they drove off, shuddering as he watched. Kent whispered the words "For you Bobby, for you my boy..."

When Cleeve was done relating his parts of the story of that night he and I looked at each other, staring intently into each other's eyes for a few moments.

"Would you have killed him?" I asked. "You had the chance after all..."

Cleeve looked at my cock as it hung out of my underpants and seemed to take in the fact that it had gone semi rigid.

"No," he said softly and folded his arms over his massive chest. "He was a worthy adversary. He cut my partner's face, but he was a worthy adversary, and for that reason I'm sorry he's gone. He deserved better than cancer..."

That said Cleeve took a few steps away from the post he had been leaning against.

"You want another drink Doc?" Cleeve asked me.

"No," I replied curtly. "What I want is to know why I'm here talking to you Cleeve. This isn't your style. Why did you kidnap me instead of Bobby? I'm guessing you and Otis saw us in front of my office. The chance to snare Bobby again after all these years..."

"I wanted you! OKAY DOC? I WANTED YOU!!" Cleeve suddenly thundered at me, his eyes, if they were daggers would have pierced me.

Suddenly I understood, or at least I prayed I understood...

"Cleeve, you chose me over Bobby for a reason..." I said, trying my best to sound like a psychiatrist and not a man who feared for his life at the moment. "Is there something you want to tell me? Something you want, or need, to talk about..."

In response he simply looked at me, trying to stare through me it seemed. I needed to coax him on. It was at that moment that I wanted to find out what it was that had made this man the way he was. What had caused Cleeve to become the sadistic and vicious man that he was today? I had already been able to gather from what Master Kent and Bobby had told me that Otis was a follower. From what I could tell it was Cleeve who was the brains behind kidnapping innocent men and torturing them. But then of course the question that begged to be asked there was, "How did Cleeve manage to get Otis to go along with the things he wanted where these men were concerned? Somehow I had to pry it out of Cleeve and looking at him as I sat there tied up wearing just my underpants I somehow got the feeling that he wanted to tell me. My cock betrayed me by growing stiffer yet. I had to laugh at that, seeing as when I was much younger I never had a problem rising to the occasion after I had shot a load or a few. Otis had sucked me off not all that long ago and now, at a much greater age here I was acting like a young man and growing hard all over again. Again I saw Cleeve take in the sight of my manhood.

"Just tell me one thing Cleeve, one thing and we'll go from there," I said softly.

"What thing do you mean Doc?" Cleeve asked in response.

"Anything you want to say, just say it," I said. "Try something that you've never said before...to anyone..."

"Why are you doing this?" Cleeve asked me and I simply stated that I believed he chose me because he wanted my help.

Again he looked at me blankly...

"Say anything Cleeve...something you've never said before... say..." I began.

"I heard my father screaming," Cleeve said, cutting me off in mid sentence. "I FUCKING HEARD MY FATHER SCREAMING!!!!"

His shout was anger, total and animalistic rage, years and years of pent-up fury. He shouted it again, "I HEARD MY FATHER SCREAMING!!!" and this time he punched the wall.

"Why was your father screaming Cleeve?" I asked. "Had you done something wrong?"

"Something wrong?" Cleeve chuckled and for a moment turned away from me as he rubbed his hand with the other where he'd punched it against the wall. "It should have been that simple, that the ten year old boy did something wrong and that was why his father was screaming!"

My jaw dropped for a moment as I took in this information.

"Ten years old Cleeve?" I asked him softly. "What did your father do to you when you were ten years old?"

Cleeve hunkered down in front of me and took my semi hardness in hand, handling it almost lovingly, making me breathless. Cleeve chuckled again as he stroked me a few times and said that his father had never done anything to him, nothing bad.

"He was the best father a boy could have asked for," Cleeve said, looking up into my eyes as he held my cock in hand. "Bobby was lucky Doc. He found Master Kent. Master Kent took care of that kid and from what I saw tonight when he was talking with you outside your office he turned out to be a great man. If Bobby is a leather master now and if he has a boy that boy is lucky too... *Bobby was lucky...* My father died when I was ten years old Doc...just like Bobby's parents. I was just a little kid when my father died. Hard to believe that I and that boy share such a bond...and I tortured him..."

So whatever it was that made Cleeve's father scream and then his eventual death all occurred when Cleeve was ten years old. I had gone this far. I had to get the rest out of him. I took a deep breath and said, "Okay Cleeve, your father didn't do anything to you. So what happened to *him*?" Cleeve let go of my cock and stood straight up, looking down at me. His eyes seemed to fill with tears for a moment but he managed to quickly pull them back.

"Tell me Cleeve," I said as soothingly as possible.
Cleeve looked at me, leaned against the post again and said, "I was powerless to help him, I was just a kid..." I pursed my lips together and still feeling his hand as it held my cock I took a deep breath. "Doc, I was so scared, so fucking scared that night. But it was the last time I would ever be scared..."

"Tell me," I said.

Cleeve began by telling me that his mother worked as a runway model, that she was extraordinarily beautiful, and on the night that he was about to relate to me she was away in Italy on a photo shoot for a women's fashion magazine. I asked him what his father did for a living and a chill went through me when he said that he owned the construction company "Green and Sons", the same company that Bobby used to work for, the same company that a few of Cleeve and Otis' other victims had worked for... I was in total shock at that moment...

"*You* own Green and Sons?" I asked Cleeve softly, totally breathless.

"I suppose you might say that I'm like the absentee landlord," Cleeve said. "I own it and it's the only part of my life where I use my real name..."

Now it all made sense, how Cleeve was able to snag the guys

off the jobsites so easily, how he picked and chose certain men. It also made sense how he had achieved such wealth. His father had made the business into what it was, no doubt Cleeve's mother had the right people running it as the boy grew up and when Cleeve was of age he inherited it all.

"So it's all yours?" I asked. "No siblings to share it with?"

"No, I was an only child," Cleeve responded. "My parents had talked about maybe having a second at some point, but with my mother's job as a model and constantly working she really needed to keep her figure…as they say…"

I nodded and looked at Cleeve expectantly, silently willing him to continue with what he was about to tell on the night he heard his father screaming.

"It was about two AM when I heard the sound of a man scream and then him grunting in pain," Cleeve began. "That was what I meant when I said that I heard my father screaming. That sound was followed by a second grunt of pain and the sound of a piece of furniture falling over. Till this day it amazes me that no one who lived under us heard the sound of a night table being thrown over. We owned a three bedroom condo in a luxury building at the time. When I heard the third sound of a man grunting in pain I decided to investigate."

Cleeve said that he threw back the sheet and slowly got out of bed. It was a warm night, not warm enough for air conditioning though, so he in his room and his dad in the master bedroom were sleeping with the windows cracked open. In his slipper feet Cleeve silently opened the door to his bedroom and walked noiselessly toward his father and mother's bedroom, only the tiny nightlight that his parents left on in the short hallway illuminating his way for him. As Cleeve approached his parents bedroom he heard the sound of a fist connecting with a jaw and then his father's voice saying, "Fucking bastards!! You'll do best to get the fuck outa here and be on your merry ways now…" Then the sound of a man as he landed on the floor. Somehow Cleeve knew not to make a sound as he cautiously approached the bedroom. He saw that the door to his parent's bedroom was slightly cracked open, just enough for a person to peek in with one eye. The bedroom was bathed in the light from the lamp on his mother's night table, the one that hadn't been overturned. As Cleeve peered into the room he saw his father, a handsome, muscle bound godlike Hercules sprawled on the floor on his back. Standing over him were three burly men, all of them clad in jeans and tee shirts, the muscles in their arms the size of bowling balls, their shoulders wide as doorways. With one hand Cleeve's father was cupping his chin, trying to rub away the pain that had been dealt him when he had been slugged those three times that Cleeve had just mentioned. As Cleeve peered into the room he heard the first of the three guys ask, "Where's that pretty model wife of yours Mr. Nelson?" and the boy's heart thundered in his chest in total fear. The three men had obviously made their way up the fire escape to Cleeve's parent's bedroom window. Upon finding the window slightly opened to let in fresh air during the night made it very easy for them to get into the apartment. However, not finding Cleeve's beautiful mother there made their plot not all that easy. From what Cleeve said, how the first guy asked where his mother was, one didn't need three guesses to know what they were there for. It stands to reason that these men knew Cleeve's mother, more than likely they even lived near or around the area where Cleeve and his parents lived. From my experience as a psychiatrist and dealing with rape victims I've found that nine out of ten times the victims know their attackers...

"My wife, what the fuck do the three of you monsters want with my wife?" Cleeve's father snarled angrily, hefting himself up on his elbows.

"Ha, as if you need three guesses Big boy," the second guy asked in reply, reached down and grabbed a handful of the man's tee shirt that he had been sleeping in.

"UUURRRRHHHHH" Cleeve's father grunted as he was yanked to his knees, his tee shirt being shorn along the way, revealing some of his muscular chest and one of his big fleshy silver dollar sized nipples.

He made a fist, ready to defend himself, but the third guy beat him to it, slamming his own fist quickly into the back of Cleeve's father's neck.

"HOOOOFFFFFFF!!!!" he heaved and his head spun.

The second guy let go of Cleeve's father's tee shirt and the man was again sprawled on the floor, this time on his side as he looked up at the three men. "Fucking dirty fighters..."

"Search the place for her," the first guy said to his two cohorts.

"N-no, no, no need to search," Cleeve's father said, again hefting himself to his elbows.

His hugest fear, obviously, was that they would find the ten year old Cleeve and do to him what they had planned on doing with his mother.

"She isn't here...she's away on assignment..." Cleeve's father stammered miserably. "I-I'm here by myself...so the three of you wasted your time...and...HOOOFFFFFFF!!!!"

The man's words were cut short by a booted foot kicking him meanly in the ribs. Cleeve's father wrapped his arms around his lower stomach area and heaved more heavily, gasping out the words, "The jokes on you, you fuckers, she ain't here..."

Cleeve stopped speaking for a moment and looked at me.

"I thought quickly to call the police," he said softly. "But they had cut the telephone wire. And back then there was no such thing as cell phones..."

"So, the way I'm gathering this, your father was asleep when those three men made their way into his bedroom window..." I said sounding deeply saddened.

"Yeah, somehow they knew my mother," Cleeve said. "Looking back on it over the years I wondered if the three lowlifes worked for my dad in his construction company. My dad always bragged how his wife was a model and showed off the pictures of her in the fashion magazines. The overturned night table was the sound that had awakened me, and my father's screaming of course. When it woke up my dad was when the three bastards pummeled him. Being that he was more asleep than awake he wasn't able to do much to defend himself. By the time that fucker kicked him in the ribs he was totally unable to stop them from what they did next."

I looked at Cleeve and asked, although I knew, "What did they do next?"

The first guy, the biggest of the three who seemed to be the ringleader said that he doubted very much the joke was on them, seeing as they could make do with him just as well. He claimed that handsome, Adonis like men always made better sport than lovely ladies. The second guy took Cleeve's father by a handful of his hair and yanked him upwards.

"Wh-what the fuck does that mean, make do with me? OOUUCCHHH!!!" the well built man in his tee shirt and white briefs bantered as he was dragged on his hands and knees back to his queen sized bed.

The third guy picked up the glass framed 8x10 portrait of

Cleeve and his wife on their wedding day.

"Man, she sure is a beautiful piece of ass," the third guy said, sounding very street and scurvy as he said it.

Cleeve's father looked up; saw the guy holding the picture and his anger boiled to the surface again as the guy stuck out his tongue... With a lecherous look on his pock marked and scarred face the guy slid the tip of his mangy tongue over the side of the picture where Cleeve's mother was depicted, twirling his tongue tip over the crotch area of her wedding gown.

"You fucker, you goddamned pervert put that down!!" the man growled and the first guy grabbed the picture from his buddy and whacked Cleeve's father over the head with the glass frame, the sound of the frame shattering. "OOWWWWWWW!!!"

The glass rained down the sides of his head and he muttered the words, "Holy fuck..."

Cleeve looked at me woefully and said, "They hit my father over the head with his wedding picture, can you believe that shit Dr. Carlson?"

"Why didn't you run to a neighbor for help?" I asked him.

"I was terrified, it seemed I was literally rooted to the spot," Cleeve replied. "I was afraid they would hear me and if they did I thought they would kill my father..."

His response made sense, the way a ten year old boy's would...

"They knew your mother but they didn't know that your parents had a son," I said, noting that the three men made no move or threat against the ten year old Cleeve.

"Apparently not," Cleeve said agreeably. "Which was also why he didn't want them to search the apartment, somehow I got the feeling that he knew I had heard the ruckus and that I was awake."

"Did he know you were watching the shattering spectacle as it unfolded in his room?" I asked.

In response Cleeve only stared at me...

After the first guy had whapped Cleeve's father over the head with the picture frame he dragged the Herculean guy over to the bed by the handful of his hair, Cleeve's father crawling along on his hands and knees, gasping in pain, the other two men taking in the sight of his round bubble butted cheeks as they pointed straight up in the air...

"C'mon along Doggy, c'mon Mr. Nelson, you're about to become our pussy for the night…" the first guy laughed and looked over at his two buddies. "Trigger, Jason, get the wire off that fallen lamp. We'll use it to tie Tarzan here to the bed with…"

"Aw no, no, you guys wouldn't…" Cleeve's father pleaded through clenched teeth.

"Its that or we knock you out and search the apartment for that lovely wife of yours muscle head…you make the choice…" the first guy said and pulled up hard on the handful of Cleeve's father's hair, yanking him up toward his bed.

"OOOWWWWWWRRR!!!" the man snarled and landed on his bed in a heap of muscles.

He turned over quickly when the first guy let go of his hair, ready to finally defend himself, but as he sat up, from behind him the third guy meanly whacked him over the head a second time with the shattered glass frame.

"YARRRHHHHH!!!" Cleeve's dad railed and landed on his back on the bed, his hands automatically covering his crown.

When Cleeve stopped speaking again momentarily I asked him, "Your last name is Nelson?"

"Yeah, Nelson," Cleeve said.

I nodded and let him continue…

They got Cleeve's father tied to the bed in the most embarrassing of positions. His arms were spread wide in front of him and lamp wire was wound around and around his massive sized wrists and the slack of it was tied off to the sides of the bed board. With him now up on his knees they meanly shredded his white briefs off him followed by tearing away the rest of his tee shirt. Mr. Nelson stared through the slats in the bed board as the man named Trigger wedged an arm around his stomach area.

"Upsadaisy Tarzan," Trigger laughed as he hefted the god-like man's ass high and the guy named Jason spread his legs out wide, widely enough so that his rosebud of an asshole was gaping flauntingly and on total display.

"Fuck man, lookit the goddamned lips of that shit chute," the first guy, the nameless one said as he shucked off his work boots and began sliding his jeans down his massively muscled legs. "This guy is cherry you two…we hit a goldmine here! That hole is gonna be tighter than any pussy on God's green Earth tonight…"

"Yeah, who needed his wife after all huh?" Trigger asked, as he and Jason followed suit in stripping off their work boots and jeans.

"You bastards, this is humiliating," Cleeve's father railed on the bed, his head turned as he watched his captors stripping down.

When they de-under-panted Cleeve's father's eyes opened wide in mortal fear at the sizes of the three men's flagpole like cocks...

"Holy smacks, untie me you faggots!!" Mr. Nelson railed, his head still turned as he took in the massive girth and width of the three men's tools.

With his head turned he also happened to notice the very thin image of a little boy at his slightly opened bedroom door.

"Aw no, no, NO!!!" Cleeve's father ranted, trying harder to get himself untied while at the same time shaking his head in a motion of "Go away, go away..."

But Cleeve stood, as he said, rooted to the spot...

"Here, let me gag the guy for you buddy," Jason said, using a piece of Mr. Nelson's torn underpants to fill his mouth with, a shred of his tee shirt over them, jamming them in his mouth.

"RRRRMMMFFFF..." Cleeve's father ranted and dug his knees deeper into the sheets of his bed, causing his sexy ass to move higher yet.

"Good idea Jason, the way I'm about to de-virginize that hole of his he's gonna be screaming bloody murder..." the first guy laughed as he stroked his hardness up to a massive sized steely erection.

Cleeve's father watched in horror as the guy spit a few times into his hand and slicked up his monster of a cock. Then, he climbed up on the bed behind his captured prey...

"RHO, RHO," Mr. Nelson pleaded, trying to say "No", knowing that his young son was seeing this.

But then, Cleeve's father saw stars and his hole felt as if a pile driver drill had suddenly entered it. The nameless guy slid all nine to ten inches of his pole right into Mr. Nelson's most private hovel.

"GGGRRRRRRMMMMFFFFFFFF!!!!" Mr. Nelson roared as his hole was assaulted and the guy started thrusting, fucking and reaming him savagely.

"Oh yeah you stud, if your model wife could see you now..." the guy whispered in Mr. Nelson's ear, chewing on his earlobe in between filling his anal cavity with his massive meat pole.

"GGGGRRRRRRFFFFFF RHOOOOO RODDDDD!!!!" Cleeve's father cried, his head arched back as he ranted, trying to say, "Oh

God!!" as he was mercilessly fucked.

From the door Cleeve watched in a state of shock mixed with horror as his poor dad struggled in his bonds with something the size of an over-ripe cucumber wedged inside him.

The bed rocked up and down as the guy made like he was on a pogo stick behind Mr. Nelson...

As the time passed Cleeve didn't move from his vantage point as he watched the three men taking turns using his dad as if he was a cheap whore on a Saturday night. Each time one of them pile drove inside him Cleeve's father screamed in agony. It seemed that no matter how much his hole was stretched he just could not comfortably accommodate his three captor's hugeness.

"Hurry it up Jason, you've been pounding him long enough," Trigger said as he stood by the bed with a new hard-on dripping pre cum between his legs. "I'm about ready for another round of porking the tar outa this guy..."

"mmmmfffff..." Mr. Nelson whispered miserably, his face buried in his pillow, filled more with agony for what his ten year old son was witnessing than for all the pain he was enduring.

"Fuck off Trigger," Jason cackled as he rode Mr. Nelson's ass like it was a pony, his cock buried so deep that he muttered how he could feel Tarzan's squishy shit. "This hole is like a velvet glove, and I plan to fill it again...FUCKING A!!!"

"Gentlemen, we have all night...no need for any of us to rush..." the ringleader said, his cock thrust up and hard yet again, even after having plowed the poor guy tied to the bed two times already.

By the time each of the men had fucked him three times each Mr. Nelson was only semi conscious and at that point only dimly aware of the pain he was being dealt. Once Cleeve's father was quiet and no longer struggling they took the gag out of his mouth and untied him from the bed.

"Time for new positions for our muscle head here," the first guy laughed as he hauled the well-fucked Mr. Nelson off the bed. "Get that night table righted up..."

"ooooooooooohhhhhhhh..." Mr. Nelson moaned as he was lifted off the bed and dropped unceremoniously on his back atop the upturned night table.

The first guy grabbed the giant man's legs from behind him, his own naked ass hanging in Mr. Nelson's face and hefted his muscular legs way up, opening up his cum sopped hole for more butt breaking thrusts. It amazed Cleeve's father how the three young men were able to fuck him so deep, cum like crazy each time and then be rejuvenated again while their buddies went to town on him.

As the first thug held Mr. Nelson's legs up and spread he sat on the man's face. Cleeve's father was forced to sniff what he called "the rotten eggs" of his rapist's hole. The sounds of laughter, the scents of cum and the moans of a man in agony filled the bedroom...

When it was the first guy's turn again at bat he re-tied Cleeve's father, binding his arms behind him. Then, he forced the guy to stand up as he took position behind him this time... Humiliation and disgrace filled the all-macho construction worker as his own hard-on was revealed. As the guy slid his cock into Cleeve's fathers butt-hole for what felt like the umpteenth time that night the guy wrapped his strong arms tightly around the man and hoisted him up off the floor.

"URRRRHHHHHHH..." Cleeve's father bellowed and involuntarily squelched his legs upward as he was bounced on the spearing cock. "you bastards..."

Mr. Nelson's hard cock bounced and flounced from side to side as the nameless thug fucked and porked his cum sopped hole. Looking up at the ceiling as he was hoisted up and down on the monstrosity as it stretched his hole with each pounding Cleeve's father clenched his teeth and held back his tears of both agony and rage. Somehow, inside him he knew that Cleeve witnessing this awful spectacle would be ruined for life...not to mention how his hole would never be the same either.

A short while later the three men proved their agility as they double fucked the helpless brawny construction worker. The first guy lay down on the night table with his hard cock pointing straight up while Trigger positioned himself at the first guy's dangling legs and Jason at his head as it rested atop the night table.

"Oh man, this is gonna be fucking searing HOT bliss..." Trigger chortled as he and Jason hefted the helpless construction worker between the two of them by his ankles and arms.

Slowly, Mr. Nelson was lowered onto the first guy's erection and Trigger's as he sidled his hardness next to his buddies...

"What the fuck??? Oh what the fuck are you guys doing now???" Cleeve's father panted almost hoarsely. "Hey...put me down...oh shit..."

A loud slurping sound was heard as the twin hard-ons were rammed meanly and savagely up Cleeve's father's rectal cavity.

"AAAARRRRRRRHHHHH, Oh my Gawd, no, no, not two at the same time," Mr. Nelson shrieked and this time his tears did flow. "OH GOD, this is new levels of pain you psychos!"

The three men laughed meanly...

Finally, Cleeve stopped and looked at me forlornly. He finished the story of his father's rape by telling me how it had gone on practically all night. The three men even used his father's mouth when they needed to piss. They made him lick their sweaty assholes. When they couldn't get their cocks up any longer because of all the times they had fucked the poor man they started taking turns fisting him. It was awful. They would force their entire fist in his hole, prod him till he couldn't see straight and then make him lick all the slick refuse from his raunchy hole off their hands. By the time they exited the bedroom the same way they had come Cleeve's father was one beat to shit guy. They left laughing as they climbed down the fire escape, leaving Mr. Nelson unbound on the floor of his ransacked bedroom. Breathing heavily, his head spinning, his mouth tasting like a urinal and his hole leaking and dribbling cum Cleeve's father crawled across the room toward the door, gasping his son's name...

"When he opened the door I was no longer there," Cleeve said.

"Where had you gone?" I asked him.

"Back to my room..." Cleeve answered. "I pretended I was asleep. "My father was more worried about my well being, so worried that he didn't even go to the hospital. He peeked into my room and I think that somehow he convinced himself that he had imagined seeing me there at his door while those three bastards worked him over."

Mr. Nelson sobbed awfully as he made his way to the bathroom and climbed into a hot shower.

"How do you feel now that you've told me this Cleeve?" I asked the man who had taken me and so many others before me prisoner.

"I don't know Doc," Cleeve said. "I mean, I've carried this around with me all my life. So I suppose it seems right that I told it to you."

"How so does it seem right?" I asked him, hoping he would say what I thought he would say.

"Bobby was one of my and Otis' victims twenty years ago at

this point," Cleeve said. "Tonight I see Bobby again for the first time in twenty years...and he's with you, a psychiatrist. I see that as fate. I had wanted to explore myself and then there you were a psychiatrist with one of my victims from the distant past. All my life that night of my father's rape plagued me and then Bobby somehow brings you to me. I find out that me and that boy had much in common...and I tortured him...I tortured that boy. And now I unload my demons on that boys' psychiatrist. It seems fitting somehow."

I nodded. In a way Cleeve had been right. It seemed as if fate had most definitely stepped in that night twenty years later and brought him and me together.

"How did your father seem to you the next morning?" I asked him.

"Well, that was when my mother returned from her trip to Italy," Cleeve said. "She actually got home while he and I were still in bed... The magazine she had done the photo shoot for sent her home on an overnight flight, a red-eye..."

Cleeve said that his father acted as if nothing had happened. Cleeve's mother didn't notice that the lamp on her husband's night table no longer had a wire attached to it. Cleeve's father had thrown away the lamp wire that the three thugs had used to bind him with. As for the broken frame of the wedding picture, Cleeve's father explained that off as having knocked it over during the night when he had gotten up to use the bathroom. He told his wife that he had been more asleep than awake and he had accidentally knocked it over. The family had breakfast together that morning and a few times while they were eating Mr. Nelson looked suspiciously over at his son. Cleeve revealed nothing. Except for a slight limp in his walk Mr. Nelson showed no tell-tale signs of his horrid experience. The mark on his face from being thwacked he told his wife was from having fallen out of bed during the night. She seemed to accept this explanation.

"Two days later my father was dead Doctor Carlson," Cleeve said, stunning me further yet. "I found him. He'd hung himself in the bedroom. He used one of his belts to do it with."

"*My God...*" I whispered.

Cleeve went on to say how his mother never knew the reason for her husband's suicide.

"You mean to say that all your life you kept that inside you?" I asked him. "You never told anyone that story, not even Otis?"

In response Cleeve shook his head, "no."

It all made sense now from a therapeutic point of view. By keeping the demons of the night of his father's rape inside him Cleeve was never able to let go of the horrid memories. In my best estimation the man became the thing he hated the most. He became those three men, hunting down and torturing innocent men. And seeing as all three of the thugs were on the muscular side it made sense that the men Cleeve chose for his and Otis' escapades also are on the muscular side.

"What about Otis?" I asked Cleeve.

"What about him?" Cleeve asked in reply.

"How did you and he come to be?" I went on. "I mean, how is it possible that not just one, but two, two men could want this same thing, this thing being to abduct and torture men..."

"Otis worked for my construction company years ago when I first took it over," Cleeve responded. "Before I met him I had already abducted a number of men and worked them over. I never felt the need for a partner. Just like in the Batman movie where he was reluctant at first to take Robin on as a partner. But then he falls for the young guy because they had so much in common, both of them having lost their parents at a young age that is."

"Did you fall for Otis?" I asked.

Cleeve laughed sarcastically and said, "No." He explained how he and Otis did have manly sex once in a while just to satiate each other but no, he was not now and never had been in love with Otis. Cleeve went on to tell me how he was straight. He did not desire men in the sense of a gay man. What Cleeve wanted was to avenge his father through the men he captured, the same way that Bruce Wayne became Batman to avenge his parent's murder, although Cleeve took the opposite direction that the fictional character of Bruce Wayne took. As stated, Otis worked for Green and Sons, a few years before the two men's paths would bring them to Bobby. Cleeve found Otis in a men's room with another guy. The lanky but muscular Otis had somehow managed to force another of the male workers up against a wall and overpower him. As Cleeve approached the men's room he heard the sounds of "You goddamned bastard!!" emanating from within. For the briefest of moments memories of that horrid night when he was ten years old played in his tormented mind. Cleeve burst into the men's room, expecting to see the three men who had brutally raped his father all those years ago. What he saw instead was that Otis had one of the other workers propped up against a urinal. The man was literally standing in the wall length urinal, his booted feet sopped with piss. The guy was a handsome boyish looking dude in his mid to upper thirties, what Cleeve and Otis at the ages they were at at that time would have considered an older guy. The guy's arms were strapped up behind him with Otis' belt and as Cleeve walked into the bathroom Otis was at that moment lowering the guy's worn jeans from behind.

"What in the fuck is going on in here?" Cleeve ranted at the sight before him.

"Fuck, I thought I had locked that damned door..." Otis complained turning and seeing Cleeve.

"He fucking hit me over the head and tied me up like this Mr. Nelson," the guy standing in the urinal yelled.

"Fucking liar!" Otis retorted.

Otis pleaded his case by telling Cleeve that the guy wanted this, that this was his fantasy that he had told to Otis in the strictest of confidences. The guy again called Otis a fucking liar. Cleeve made Otis free the guy and send him on his way. To make up for what had happened and to avoid charges being pressed against the construction company Cleeve gave the worker three weeks off with pay plus a salary bonus. Then he dealt with Otis.

"Is this what *you* like too Mr. Briggs?" Cleeve asked Otis, after having found out his last name. "You like subduing guys and making them beg for mercy? You like having studly fuckers at your feet?"

As Cleeve spoke he grabbed Otis by the throat and slammed him against a wall, stunning the other man.

"UUUHHHFFFF..." Otis gasped at the sudden onslaught.

"I like it too Briggs, but I'll tell you this you fucking moron and a half," Cleeve seethed in the man's face. "I WILL NOT have my company put at risk to feed my or anyone else's fantasies! Do I make myself clear on all that?"

Otis said it was perfectly clear but then in a sarcastic tone asked the company owner if he planned on firing him, stating how with this little incident on his record it would be nearly impossible for him to find any future construction work.

"Fire you? You don't get what I'm trying to tell you here do you, you stupid stack of shit?" Cleeve asked and loosened his hold on Otis' neck. "I'm offering you a way of keeping your job AND helping me at the same time. Didn't you hear what I said to you? I like what you like too Briggs, only I think I like it a lot more than you do!"

Cleeve told Otis how he had purchased a huge old mansion-like house in a remote area of upstate New York and what he was planning on making the place into. He went on to tell Otis that the house was surrounded by nothing but woods. Otis liked what he heard, he liked it a lot.

"So if you really want that piece of ass that I just caught you with and then some, and I mean then some," Cleeve said, speaking now through clenched teeth. "You would best stick with me Briggs. What do you say?"

In response Otis slid to his knees and gave Cleeve what would be the first of many blow-jobs...

I looked at Cleeve, thought for a few moments and asked, "So did you and Otis go after that guy that you had caught him with in that men's room?"

"No, but we did find a guy that resembled him," Cleeve said. "And he didn't work for Green and Sons."

"So he was the first man the two of you ever abducted?" I asked.

Cleeve looked up at the ceiling and then at me.

"For Otis he was the first, for me I had already lost count at that point," Cleeve replied. "You see Doctor Carlson, the first time I ever abducted a guy I was in high school..."

So when Cleeve was a teenager his demons could no longer be kept at bay. He began what would be deemed his abduction career in a high school locker room, when he overpowered, blindfolded and raped a young man named "Bradley Richards", the captain of the high school's football team... Cleeve didn't go into graphic detail about that incident. I had heard enough to know what he must have done with the handsome and hunky high school football captain...

Cleeve and I talked all night...until the sun came up...

The next morning Otis came back down to the dungeon/basement looking refreshed and well rested. Cleeve quickly told his buddy how he and I had been talking all night and that they were not going to torture me. Otis disagreed with Cleeve's decision, touched the scar on his face but acquiesced to the man who had mentored him for so many years.

"So what are we going to do with him?" Otis asked.

"Something we never did before," Cleeve said, looking at me menacingly and my heart sank for a moment. "We're going to release him without having worked him over..."

Later that morning Cleeve's van pulled up in front of my office, where he and Otis had captured me the night before. I was dressed in my suit and tie and overcoat and sitting up front with the two men, rather than tied up in the back. Cleeve stopped the van and Otis stepped out, making the way for me to step out next.

"I want to thank you Cleeve," I said, holding out my hand for him to shake.

"More like it should be me who thanks you Doc," Cleeve replied and shook my hand.

"What are your plans?" I asked him. "If I may ask..."

Cleeve looked out of the van at Otis before he replied.

"Otis and I have been talking about traveling," Cleeve said. "We may go to England."

"To abduct men there you mean?" I asked him.

"No, just to go to England..." Cleeve said and tugged my tie. "Maybe after last night I'll finally be able to put it all behind me...who knows?"

That said Otis watched as Cleeve leaned forward and clamped his mouth down on mine, kissing me long and hard...

I stood in the street in the early morning light and watched as Cleeve and Otis drove off, their van getting smaller and smaller in my vision till I could no longer see it. I quickly dashed into my office and wrote down the license plate number of Cleeve's van...

About the Author

Christopher Trevor was born in July 1963 and grew up in New York City. As soon as he was old enough to know how he began writing fiction and has been writing gay erotic/fetish stories for the past ten to twelve years at this point. He became an avid reader as well from the time he knew how and reads everything from fiction, to non-fiction to biographies of interesting and unusual people, people who have made a difference or who have paved the way for others. Christopher attributes his writing artistic inspiration to artists such as Etienne, Tom of Finland, Tagame, The Hun, and most notably Joe T, who Christopher has had the

pleasure of speaking with and even meeting over the last few years. Christopher states, "Joe T encouraged me to write about my fetish because I was embarrassed about it at the time. Joe T said that when we are embarrassed about something that makes it even more enticing somehow." Christopher totally agreed and never stopped writing in this genre. Erotic writers who inspired Christopher Trevor were: Tom Shaw (author of "That Day at the Quarry), C.S. White (author of Big Sur), Larry Townsend (author of countless erotic novels), and Mason Powell (author of the classic story "The Brig.")

Christopher discovered that not only did he enjoy writing erotic tales but that after his first bondage experience he had a genuine flair for it. Writing to erotic oriented magazines about his first bondage experience truly opened the floodgates for Christopher where this style of writing is concerned. Christopher thanks the handsome and muscular "Greg" for that experience way back in time. Christopher took "Creative Writing" courses every semester during his high school years and while other friends of his stopped writing what they loved to write about as time went on Christopher never let a day go by when he didn't write something... "I feel that if I don't write every day I will die," Christopher has said many times over.

Foot fetish stories and all things related; spanking fetish, erotic shaving, muscle bondage, tickle torture, and hardcore stories are just a few of the areas of gay eroticism that Christopher enjoys writing about and inspiring in others as well. As one internet buddy said to Christopher where the black socks fetish is concerned, "Until I started talking with you I never gave a thought to my socks when I got dressed for work in the morning. Now when I pull my dress socks on every morning I get a chill up my spine."

Christopher is proud of the erotic effect he has on people...

Christopher Trevor is also the author of:

The Executive Guide to Foot Fetishism and Office Discipline
1-887895-36-1

Executive Ties That Bind
1-887895-37-X

Don't!! Stop!! That Tickles!!
1-887895-31-0

The Taming of Dominick
1-887895-45-0

Timmy and The Hong Kong Tailor
1-887895-30-2

Milked
978-1-88789566-8

Timmys Ticklish Trials
978-1-887895-74-3

The Gym Instructor
978-1-887895-44-6

Erotic Street Blues
978-1-887895-97-2

Look for them where you found this book or Goodboner.com.

www.ingramcontent.com/pod-product-compliance
Lightning Source LLC
Chambersburg PA
CBHW071220260626
47162CB00004B/1374